A DASH OF DISGUISE

A Lady's School for Spies
Regency Romantic Suspense Series
Book 1

Jacki Delecki

A Dash of Disguise

Copyright © 2022 by Jacki Delecki

Print Edition

Excerpt from A Code of Love © 2014 by Jacki Delecki

ISBN: 978-1-737855-47-7

Published by Doe Bay Publishing, Seattle, Washington.

For Erica—a beautiful caring woman and
a wonderful welcome to our family!

"No war can ever be conducted without good and
early intelligence."
Duke of Marlborough

Prologue

June 1799

"I NEED YOU so badly." Dash slowly unbuttoned Perdita's dress, trailing kisses along her neck from behind, his large hands caressing her breasts when her dress fell away. After being apart for over several months, Dash was voracious and demanding. Perdita gloried in this new Dash who had always treated her cautiously and gently, like the innocent she was. Today he treated her like a desirable woman.

"Being away from you, sitting indoors every day listening to professors drone on about ancient philosophers was torture worse than the Inquisition." His words rasped across her neck, causing her knees to tremble. "Why do we spend our youth listening to old men? We should be living."

She didn't understand how he was capable of thought. She was a bundle of sensations. And when he pinched her nipples, she was unable to breathe.

Perdita blushed when he turned her around to stare at her breasts, barely covered by her chemise.

"We should be enjoying beauty like yours, not listening to dried-up men. I wanted you every minute I was away." His voice roughened.

Heat danced along her skin, and her breasts grew heavy. Dash always had this effect on her. Even before he first kissed her, all it took was one look, and she was filled with longing.

She tried to focus on Dash's words, wanting to appear sophisticated, like the London women he knew. As if standing in her chemise in a field having a conversation was a normal occurrence for her. Dash had a lot more experience since he was capable of speech when she could barely stand. "You're almost finished with university. You just have to sit for your exams."

And although Dash complained about school, he was a scholar and a mathematical genius. She could never beat him at cards. Roddy, her brother, always bragged about how Dash could beat anyone in the clubs they frequented in London. She had once made the mistake of asking about the women in London's clubs. Roddy took on his supercilious tone as only older brothers mastered. "We are both to be earls. What do you think? Women fall into our laps."

It hurt to think of Dash with other women in his lap—sophisticated worldly women who loved fashion and high society. Perdita cared little about fashion. She loved her worn riding breeches, allowing her freedom to move.

"I'm selfish. I want every minute with you, Perdita. I don't want to watch you dance with other men, have men flirt with you next Season. I want to be the only man who touches you." He turned her in his arms.

She felt the same. She didn't want anyone near him now that she knew the thrill of undressing for him and what was to come next.

Perdita's season had been postponed when her mother had died as the preparations began. Her mother had caught a chill and never recovered. Perdita missed her, but in a distant way. Her mother had never been very maternal. And then, after the year of mourning, Perdita should have had a debut this last spring. Her father had instead sent her off to Miss Danvers' School for Ladies in Bath. It was the best thing to happen to Perdita; her whole world expanded. As her world was perfect now with the promise in Dash's kisses and touch.

"Do you know how gorgeous you are? I want to see you completely naked, like a pagan goddess spread out before me on the blanket."

His eyes raked over her body as his breath quickened. A flush spread over his sculpted cheekbones, making his dark eyes shine brighter. A large man, his black hair and eyes were a dramatic contrast against his fair skin. He swore he was a mix of Viking and Norman invaders. She could believe it. Dash was fierce and fearless, like his ancestors. The first time he came home with Roddy from Eton, he was a sullen and angry boy who thought girls were below him. Perdita had taught him a few lessons on girls' superiority over the years. Dash had become her best friend in all adventures.

"Take off your chemise."

Breathtakingly new but scary at the same time. She never showed any caution in the company of Dash. They rode to the hounds, practiced martial arts together, and played cards and billiards. Perdita was as competitive as Dash. They thrived on challenging each other. Winning didn't matter as much as the contest.

But this was new, this demand to be naked, and a niggling caution crept up. She had allowed him liberties, but she had always kept her clothes on. Was she ready to take this next step? She loved him, but Totty, the housekeeper, had explained why her mother had had so many "friends."

"Do you love me, Dash? Or is this just lust? Totty told me that my mother confused lust for love. I don't want to be like my mother, but I do want to be naked with you. Is that lust?" It was good that Dash was her best friend, and now… she didn't have a word for what he was now. He wasn't courting her exactly. But on his last school break, he had changed everything between them. He'd kissed her and touched her, and she could never go back to thinking of him as only a friend.

Now instead of riding or stick fighting, they spent all their time kissing and touching and gazing into each other's eyes as if they had just discovered each other. They laughed at everything and anything. The sky was brighter; Totty's baking tasted better. Perdita had never felt this euphoric. She was in love.

"Darling, I've loved you since you were eight years old and mounted a terrifying, head-throwing, stomping new palomino mare. You clung onto her mane and announced loudly that her name was Buttercup since she was the color of the flower."

He loved her. She wanted to prove how much she loved him. She lowered the straps of her chemise. Her fingers shook at the sudden loss of oxygen in the air. She couldn't look at Dash. A flush started at her toes and spread through her body. Her skin tingled in anticipation, and her heart was off like the new filly in their yard.

She let the chemise drop to the blanket on the grass. And she finally looked up at Dash. His face was filled with joy. His eyes, bright with love and hunger, would always be etched in her soul.

"Am I the only one to be naked?" she teased because she couldn't express how her heart overflowed with love.

He hooked his thumbs under his shirt, pulling it over his head and tossing it to the ground.

"Does this help?" The familiar sound of his laughter soothed her fear, and the challenge in the lift of his spectacular brow was enough to regain her confidence. He was chiseled male beauty, and he was all hers to touch and kiss.

She batted her eyelashes pretending to be coy. The power she wielded over Dash was exciting and heady and buoyed her confidence. She slowly slid her undergarment down, inch by inch. She lifted her chin and rejoiced watching Dash's chest tighten. His eyes dilated and his nostrils flared like her horse when pushed to the limit.

"You're trying to kill me," Dash growled. "You little tease."

Now Perdita laughed. Her soul was shining with happiness and total abandonment.

"You have to drop your drawers too. I want to see all of you. I want to touch you as you've touched me."

"Oh, my innocent darling. If I take my clothes off and you touch me, I won't keep my promise to your brother."

"You told my brother about us?" Perdita halted her game. Dread and betrayal destroying the mood. "What did you promise him?"

"I wouldn't take your virginity until we're married."

"You told Roddy that you…" She couldn't say it aloud. Saying it would make this most magical wonder disappear.

"You are joking." Suddenly, she was ready to pummel Dash for his cool-headed and clinical approach when she was reveling in this moment.

"Hold on, killer. Don't hurt me." He took her into his arms, pressing his bare chest against her breasts. The sensation was breathtaking. She rubbed against him, wanting more. Never wanting to leave his heat and the friction of her nipples against his chest hair.

"Perdita, you're making it difficult to keep my promise."

"The promise you won't take my virginity unless you marry me?"

She felt Dash's laugh resonate in her chest.

"I didn't say it aloud. But there is an unspoken rule about sisters. You don't fool around unless you plan to marry. Roddy is not stupid about what is happening between us. He can't miss the way you look at me."

"I look at you?" Perdita tried to sound indignant. It was hard to remain calm as her words caused her breasts to move against his thick mat of hair. "What about how you look at me like I'm a fresh scone that you plan to devour?"

"That's what I'm planning today… to taste you."

"What?"

"I promise you'll enjoy every second of it. And you'll beg me to do it again." Dash lifted his brow in the familiar way that challenged her.

She couldn't pretend that she understood, but the way his voice lowered and his muscles tightened against her sent sparks of fire through her.

"Oh, darling, don't look frightened. We'll go slow."

"You plan for us to marry?" She wanted Dash as her husband. She couldn't imagine a better man. He was loyal and funny and smart and so tender.

"Yes, once the old bastard kicks off. It shouldn't be too much longer, considering his last doctor's visit. I would never subject you to him. He'd probably try to seduce you."

She pinched the hair on his chest, brushing her fingers against solid muscle. "You sound like Roddy. Is he as bad as our father?"

"Worse. I don't want you to ever meet him. We will marry when I'm the earl. You will be my countess."

Four weeks later

DITA HURRIED DOWN the stairs into the courtyard after receiving the news that Dash was riding up the drive. She was an excited mix of anticipation and resentment, and underneath the swirling emotions was terror. She had been on tether hooks waiting for some sign after the intimacies and the promises they shared. Something was wrong. She knew it. Not only by the fact that she hadn't heard from him in over a month. She felt panic deep in her bones.

She and Dash had an unspoken connection that defied explanations. They had forged a bond as lonely youths, spending hours together, filling the empty spaces in their hearts. He hadn't communicated with either her or Roddy since his father's sudden death.

She had wanted to attend the funeral, but with no familial connection, she had remained at home. She and Roddy had argued, and she would have defied her brother except for his valid insight that a scandal was not the way to go forward for her and Dash's relationship.

He had to be hurting, which made her hurt too. She wanted to be his comfort, the solace in his sadness. And no matter how badly a parent treated a child, they still grieved. Grieved and blamed themselves that there had been no love. She understood the self-recrimination wrapped in the grief.

She ran outside as he dismounted his horse. She halted and didn't jump into his arms as she had planned. The set of his rigid jaw, stiff stance, and cool gaze kept her standing in place. The angry defiant boy was back but far more intimidating as an overpowering tense male. She didn't say anything but pleaded with her eyes, wanting warmth to shine from the icy cold orbs.

"Lady Perdita, if you would grant me a moment of your time?

Can we walk in the garden?"

She wanted to shout and scream, but a shred of self-preservation and dignity stopped her as she crumbled inside.

"May I offer my condolences at your loss."

Dash's snort gave her a moment of hope until he raised his arm imperiously for her to go ahead of him, not touching her or embracing her. She straightened her spine and lifted her chin in defiance in the way her *grandmere* had described the French royalty had walked to the guillotine. She refused to beg or plead or allow him to see her defeated. She loved him, but she'd learned from both her parents that it didn't matter how much you loved someone when you couldn't make them love you back. And a familiar feeling of being unlovable swamped her.

They walked in silence down the gravel path, heading to a private nook in the garden where they had played. It was their favorite place to hide from Totty, the nannies, and Alfie, the stable master. The sun hid behind the clouds, making her chilled, but it was the detached man who stared straight ahead, keeping at least three feet between them to avoid touching, that froze her heart.

"Why are you acting like this?" She couldn't stop herself. "Please, Dash, what is wrong? You can tell me anything." *Because I love you* wasn't said.

"Nothing is wrong, Perdita. Our childhood days are finished. We always knew we couldn't go on forever. Now that the old bastard is dead, I must assume my responsibilities, and you must take your place in society." He placed his foot on the stone bench, the place he had kissed her for the first time. With his back toward her, his arm resting on his bent knee, he assumed a careless attitude, as if he hadn't just ripped her heart out of her chest and stomped on it.

"But what of us? Your promises?" *Your promise to love me forever, to make me your wife. The tender, adoring way that you touched me.*

He was very good at hiding his feelings. His only reaction to her painful pleas was a slight flinch of his shoulders. The distance he put between them didn't change their vital connection. How could he hurt her like this when he knew how she had suffered as a girl, wanting to be loved? He never had been cruel before, only angry and uncommunicative.

"I don't understand why you can't share what is going on. Talk to me. We can work this out together."

"Perdita, grow up." He shot around, his face contorted in anger, his voice clipped. "There is no *us* now. We were childhood friends, and it is time to put it behind us."

She knew he lied. She knew that he loved her despite this act. He was in pain and was striking out. She shouldn't be surprised at his skill in hurting her. He had succeeded in wounding her as only someone who knew her well could.

"We were more than friends, and I won't let you forget our love and the passion. You made promises to me… to us."

"Darling, if you were sophisticated, you would know that men make all sorts of promises in moments of passion." The grin on his sculpted face didn't meet his eyes.

The jaded, superior tone of his endearment, combined with his accusation of her naivete, breeched her vulnerability. His hurtful attack sliced through all her walls that she had erected to protect against her parents' neglect. He didn't love her. Why should he? Her parents hadn't.

"Then we're finished here." And she ran from the garden. If she didn't leave, she would sob and plead and make a complete fool of herself, demonstrating how naïve and trusting she was.

Chapter One

April 1802

LADY PERDITA TINLEY slammed her stick against her opponent. The loud sound of smacking wood resounded against the garden walls. Alfie's subtle hesitation before shifting his weight to his right side signaled he was about to attack, and that was her cue to strike first.

She read Alfie's defense as he would anticipate her counterattack. She had been practicing her fighting skills with her father's Irish stable master since she was a girl. Dita tightened her grip and pushed forward. She had a surplus of uncontrolled emotions now that the societal pressure mounted, and stick fighting was the perfect release. Her plans for starting a school for female spies and defying society's expectations that she marry this Season fueled her fierce strikes, forcing Alfie to step back.

Alfie immediately responded to her aggression as she knew he would with a quick strike, not sparing her from retribution. Her weapon vibrated in her hands from the force of his hit. "Sparring with you must be our students' final test to ensure they have the required skills to be safe in the field."

Alfie, a man of few words, grunted. "I'll think about it when you have Lord Rathbourne's approval."

Alfie had been an outspoken opponent of her newest scheme. Once she learned from her brother that there were French spies among men and women of breeding betraying their country, she knew she had to act. The French had killed her grandfather and her uncle during the Reign of Terror and countless relatives. She wouldn't allow them to harm her family again or her country. After long hours of discussion with her classmates at Miss Danvers' School for Ladies, the plan was hatched for the school.

She'd talk Alfie around once the school was up and running. Dita laughed out loud with the sheer exhilaration of the spring sunshine, the mental and physical demands of stick fighting, and the excitement of a new beginning.

Mrs. Tottle's piercing voice halted Dita's forward motion with her stick raised to attack. "Miss Dita, you must stop immediately. Her Ladyship is in the drawing room and demands your presence."

Dita lowered her hands and turned to face the housekeeper.

"Why are you staring at me with your mouth open like a dead trout? Go change your dress and fix your hair."

Totty had been with the Tinley family since before Dita was born and still treated Dita as a child and not the mistress of the house. "Totty, what lady is in our drawing room?"

"Lady Beaumont herself. She told me to say to hasten since she doesn't have much time today before her family realizes she's escaped."

Escaped? Was Lady Beaumont, an elderly woman, losing her faculties? She'd been ill and hadn't left home for some time, but Dita hadn't heard any rumors of a decline in her mental state. And the lady had agreed to be her sponsor for the Season, which would require stamina for the late-night parties and balls.

"I was to call on her tomorrow to plan for the months ahead." Dita tucked the damp curls plastered to her cheek into her braid and smoothed the old worn dress with the relaxed seams that enabled her to swing her arms.

"It doesn't matter now. She's here. You have to make yourself presentable."

"I won't inconvenience the lady by changing. It must be important for her ladyship to have come instead of sending a message."

"You won't look respectable in that old dress," Mrs. Tottle said as an aside as she strode away, mumbling to herself about unexpected guests and whether the biscuits were still hot. She suddenly stopped and whipped around at the appearance of Dita's friend. "At least Miss Emmaline looks like a proper lady. Take her to meet her ladyship."

If Totty knew how unladylike quiet Emmaline could be, she'd have heart palpitations. Emmaline and two classmates had saved Perdita when she had been shipped to finishing school after her mother died. Her three close friends were different in appearance, disposition, and social standing, but they had become her family. The friends became inseparable. And discovered that they shared a vital connection—they all were rebels in their own ways.

In the two and half years at the school, Dita had forged a bond with the capable girls who, like herself, questioned everything and everyone. Miss Danvers had said the foursome had aged her more than any other students. But Perdita liked to believe—to avoid guilt—that their schoolmistress secretly nurtured their intellectual curiosity and tenacity, despite the school's mission to shape them for their roles as wives and mothers for the future of Great Britain. The friends had other plans for their roles for the future of their country. Each girl had personal reasons for wanting to join in the fight against France. Using their varied skills, they planned to train women to gather information for Lord Rathbourne's Office of Intelligence.

"You have a very important guest, Dita. You mustn't keep her waiting." Emmaline used her finger to push her glasses back on her nose. Poor Emmy's eyesight suffered from her constant reading. Her thick brown hair was pulled tightly into a knot at her nape, her dress modest with long sleeves and lace fichu covering any exposed skin as a good vicar's daughter should dress.

Emmy Rothsby's father was the third son of the Earl of Maylesbury, scorned by his father for having made the grave mistake of marrying below him. Emmy didn't have funds or connections to take in a London Season. A few years older, Emmy served as Dita's companion, which was perfect since her friend had no desire to mingle with her "betters" or be on the marriage mart. And Perdita needed a companion to go out into society.

"I'm sure Lady Beaumont will understand that this is not the time of day that you call upon people. Catching me unawares, she can't expect me to be dressed for a formal call." Dita quickened her pace, curious about the reason for Lady Beaumont's visit and her comment about escaping her family. Surely Emmy would have heard rumors about the lady's decline.

"Her ladyship don't have to follow any social rules. She makes them. And don't she know it. Bossing me around like I was her servant." And with the last tidbit, Mrs. Tottle hurried through the kitchen door. "I must get the tray ready."

Emmy linked arms with Dita as they headed toward the house. "It is probably better if Lady Beaumont doesn't learn of your stick fighting or any of the other techniques Alfie has instructed you in, such as knife fighting. I doubt she would find it behavior acceptable for a lady."

Alfie had traveled to the Far East before he became their stableman, then eventually the stable master. Alfie had a way with fearful animals and spirited girls. He had trained Dita in martial arts that he had learned during his time as a sailor. He had taken it upon himself to tutor her, filling her lonely days. He loved to wink and say she had a talent for finding trouble and needed to know how to extricate herself.

"I'm hoping that my connection to the lady will give me many more opportunities to engage with her nephew. Lord Rathbourne must be persuaded by the information that we've gathered on Lord Yardley that we are capable of training other women to spy for the war effort." Dita patted her curls down to try to have some semblance of propriety. "The idea of our school sounded more credible when we were hatching this mad scheme."

"We agreed that we have to try." Emmy patted her arm. "What is the worst thing that could happen?"

"Lord Rathbourne thinks we're a bunch of meddling spinsters, or Roddy finds out and forces me into a marriage for behaving in a manner unfitting to my position."

"Your brother will never force you to marry anyone."

Roddy was a good sort and would never allow her to suffer as their mother did under her husband's rule. Her mother had been desperate for attention and had sought comfort in her changing consorts. Roddy was nothing like their father but, like all men of his station, believed that a woman's only meaningful role in society was to be wife and mother. He would never condone her involvement in the war effort. He expected her to marry this Season.

"I wish I could share the truth with Lady Beaumont, who has generously volunteered to sponsor me. She only agreed to the role since she was a close friend of my grandmere. I was instructed by my grandmere that if I were ever in need I was to go to Lady Beaumont. I feel like I'm betraying them both by not confiding my real reason for participating in the Season. The poor woman believes I want to marry."

There had a been a time when Perdita planned to marry and raise dark-haired boys and girls in the likeness of a man who now resided in the deepest recesses of her heart, never to be conjured up. She hadn't seen him since the fateful day in the garden when he devastated her heart and trust. She had learned the lesson well never to trust your heart to anyone.

She doubted she'd be subjected to his presence during the Season. He'd cut all ties with his past life and withdrew from polite society once he'd obtained his title. There was a very rare chance of encountering him since he spent his time gambling and in brothels if rumors were to be believed. She refused to wonder on how many more women he had made promises to in the heat of passion.

"From the stories about your grandmother, she would want you to be involved with what matters." Emmy's green eyes flashed with resolve. "After all this planning, this is not the time for doubt."

"If our plan works, we'll owe the lady a great debt." Dita stiffened her spine and climbed the stairs to the drawing room as her friend removed herself to her sanctuary—the library.

Quickly moving, Dita surprised Billy, the footman, by opening the door to the drawing room. A stout white-haired woman, dressed in a fuchsia pelisse and matching turban with what looked like a bird's nest on the top, stood in the middle of the room. Her bright eyes were lit with warmth and intelligence. A silent sigh of relief went through Dita at Lady Beaumont's lively presence.

"Perdita, my darling girl." Lady Beaumont walked with her arms open across the large drawing room. She favored her right side slightly. But there were no other indications that the elderly woman was unwell.

The sturdy woman's arms and the scent of rosewater enveloped Dita, offering her comfort and safety as her grandmere had done. Dita bit down on her lip, fighting the tears burning behind her eyes.

"I still remember how delighted your grandmother was at your birth."

Dita clung to the comforting words. Her grandmere had loved her grandchildren. Her warmth and acceptance lessened the pain for both Perdita and Roddy from the lack of their parental attention, but she had died when they were young, leaving a gaping hole.

Lady Beaumont stepped back to look at her. "You are as lovely as your mother but with the mischievous glint of your grandmother. What fun I'll have this Season, watching you bring all the gentlemen to their knees."

Dita's throat tightened in bittersweet sadness to speak about her grandmere. "Thank you, Lady Beaumont. I have been told that I favor her in disposition." When her mother was extremely upset with her—which had been often—she would accuse her of behaving as wildly as her spirited grandmere.

"You must call me Aunt Euphemia." Lady Beaumont squeezed Dita's arm.

"It would mean a great deal to me." Dita's voice cracked with emotion.

Aunt Euphemia's eyes softened for a brief moment, and then seeming to know that Dita might embarrass herself by crying, she plopped down on the nearby settee. "I hope your housekeeper will soon bring a tea tray. I'm feeling a bit peckish. Someone from my family is going to appear before I can finish my tea."

As if on cue, Billy opened the door, allowing Mrs. Tottle to enter. Another footman carried the tray. Mrs. Tottle's gray brow was furrowed in deep worry as she supervised the footman. Lady

Beaumont's unexpected appearance discombobulated the unflappable woman.

Dita poured the tea as Aunt Euphemia piled her plate high with a biscuit, slivers of ham, cheese, and small sugar cookies.

Dita was relieved that Aunt Euphemia didn't follow the rules for a lady of breeding who must choose only a small portion and take tiny bites. Dita stacked her plate high with meats and cheese. She had worked up an appetite after her bout with Alfie.

Neither spoke but enjoyed their respite. Dita was filled with a peaceful contentment in the woman's presence. There was no artifice about Lady Beaumont, and she didn't force empty chitchat.

"It is quite wonderful to be away from Rathbourne House." Aunt Euphemia patted her lips with the white linen napkin after devouring three of the cookies. "I took a spill and had to remain off my feet for over a month with my nephew and niece hovering over me."

"I received your note, and I'm glad to see you are well. If you feel taking the Season will be a strain, I will understand. I have a distant cousin who could accompany me." Dita prayed to all the saints in heaven that she wouldn't be subjected to her odious cousin.

"I'm fit as a fiddle and looking forward to mixing in society again. The last month has been dull and boring. And I would never let my dearest friend down. We must find you an agreeable gentleman. Is there someone who has caught your fancy?"

Dita couldn't lie to this woman with honest, open eyes who also was her dear grandmere's friend. She just couldn't betray either woman. "I'm not sure I'm the marrying type of woman."

Aunt Euphemia slapped her knee and chortled loudly. "Many a woman would agree with the sentiment. I included. Is there a reason you believe such a thing? I know Annette always regretted allowing the match between her daughter and your father. The earl could be a charming man when he wanted to be. But you must not allow their unhappiness to influence your decision. There are many happy marriages based on respect and companionship."

Dita was stunned by Aunt Euphemia's frank discussion of the private lives of her parents. This wasn't the type of polite conversation made over tea. She had never told anyone outside of her school friends about the screaming fights, the accusations of infidelity between her parents. She had assumed that all couples behaved the way her parents did until she witnessed Emmy's parents' loving relationship.

And she would suffer torture before admitting to weaving dreams around a future with Dash. A future where he laughed at her jokes, challenged her to races with admiration shining in his eyes, teased her relentlessly about her lack of feminine arts. The promise of a life with someone who understood her and encouraged her. Her youthful daydreams had been packed away like her dolls and toys and sent to the attic when she outgrew them.

"Oh, I can see there is someone." Aunt Euphemia's hooded eyes were focused on Dita.

How could Perdita have considered this woman in decline? For a woman of her age, she was remarkably sharp.

"You're mistaken. I've formed no attachment to any gentleman. And I don't plan to this Season."

Her admission might have just sabotaged the plan of using the Season to gather information to prove their abilities to Lord Rathbourne.

Aunt Euphemia leaned against the back of the settee, not maintaining the straight spine required of a lady's sitting posture. "I see you're wearing Annette's necklace."

Perdita's head was spinning by the unexpected turns in conversation. Had the lady just accepted Perdita's shocking disclosure that she had no plans to marry at the ripe age of twenty-two? She had prepared herself to hear the speech that there would be a fine gentleman who would change her mind. Miss Danvers and all the teachers droned on how a woman needed protection in society. They were incapable of managing without the guidance of a husband. No man was going to convince Perdita that she needed his protection. She had learned the hard way that she had to rely on herself. She was fortunate enough to have position and money and not to need to marry.

"Did Annette explain the significance of the necklace?"

Perdita fingered the large blue sapphire in its simple silver setting. "That all the French aristocrats were trying to save themselves but didn't know who to confide in. The sapphire was a signal that the wearer could be trusted."

"Friends and family betrayed each other to survive. Sapphires were worn since notes could be intercepted and fall into the wrong hands to be used as blackmail. Sapphires have always been a symbol of trust and loyalty."

"My grandmere never liked to talk about her experiences escaping the Terror. She said it belonged in the past and no good came of remembering. She told me to always look to the future."

"She was sparing you from what she suffered. She was a brave woman. After your grandfather and your uncle were killed, Annette fought to save your mother and herself and many women whose husbands and sons were murdered."

The only time her grandmere had spoken of it was on her deathbed when she gave Perdita the necklace. But those words had inspired Perdita. The French had killed innocent people, including many of her family, and now they were planning to invade England. She wouldn't allow any other women to struggle as her grandmother through war if she could help it.

"Tell me more about her. She liked to tell me stories about her childhood but never anything later."

Totty's face was mottled and her frizzy gray hair had fallen out of her cap as she scurried into the room. "Your ladyship, Lord Rathbourne has arrived to accompany you home."

"Send my nephew away." Aunt Euphemia batted her hand in the air. "He is wasting his precious time. I'm in no need of assistance to return to Rathbourne House."

"If you were concerned about my time, you wouldn't have left home." Lord Rathbourne, a big-boned, black-haired man with severe features, hadn't waited to be announced. Knowing he was head of Intelligence, Perdita doubted he waited on anyone. Except for the King. Lord Rathbourne was humorless and rigid, and if Perdita hadn't a father who had mastered dark disapproving looks, she would be intimidated.

"Why are you the one to come for me?" Aunt Euphemia asked.

"Because I'm the only one in the family that can convince you to leave."

"Do you mean to say command?"

"Command?" Lord Rathbourne barked a loud guffaw. "No one commands you to do anything." His voice was filled with amusement and affection.

"Who ratted me out? It wasn't Henrietta. She would never betray me. Is it Gwyneth? She's got the glint in her eye that I never trust. And to think I paid her handsomely to keep my secret."

Stunned by the banter between Lord Rathbourne and his aunt, Dita finally jumped from her seat to her duties. The reason for asking Lady Beaumont to sponsor her stood before her. "Lord Rathbourne, please won't you join us for tea? Or would you prefer brandy?"

"Sit down, Cord. It is good for you to be out of your office. And knowing your habits, I can assume you haven't eaten. Your health is in jeopardy."

"You have no need to worry about my health."

"Precisely. And neither do you need to waste your time worrying about mine. I've recovered from my fall. I need to join the world. I'm making plans to sponsor the lovely Lady Perdita."

Lord Rathbourne's eyebrow raised in question at Dita. "Thank you for your hospitality, Lady Perdita, but I must return to work immediately." He glared at his aunt, who was unimpressed by his scowl and bent to butter a slice of toast.

"I understand. You bear great responsibility for England's future." Dita hesitated on how exactly to express her knowledge of the secretive role he played.

His thick brows formed a dramatic slash as his eyes narrowed on her face.

Dita hoped she didn't flinch with his piercing look. "My brother has spoken of the demands your position places on you with the war."

Roddy had said no such thing. It was fortunate he wasn't present to hear her. She couldn't admit she'd read her brother's mail when he began to act secretive, having hushed conversations in the library, letters arriving at all hours of night. At the time, she thought he had returned to his dissolute life of gambling, racing, and women. Returning to the life that he and Dash had both pursued out of university. Her worry had been ill placed; Roddy was working with the government to develop a peace plan with France.

"Men of all stations have to work to ensure the safety of our nation."

"I couldn't agree more wholeheartedly, my lord. I believe women bear the same responsibility and shouldn't be prevented from doing so."

Aunt Euphemia snickered as she stood. Her eyes were vivid with amusement and canny intelligence. "I think we are going to have a very splendid time together, my dear. You'll call on me in the next days."

Chapter Two

DASHIELL LOUIS ALEXANDER West, the Earl of Beldon, leaned against the wooden chair and took a slow draw on his cigar. His nonchalant posture belied his interest in the activities around him. The smoky club rang with the shouts of victory and dismay and the manufactured giggles of the women. The harsh cacophony was background noise for a seasoned gambler.

Haversham, the bastard son of the Duke of Leicester and the owner of the club, was engaged with a customer by the stairwell. He used his impressive bulk and misshapen nose and jaw to full effect on the frightened mouse hovering against the wall. The balding second son of a viscount, Armfield worked in a department of His Majesty's Navy, making him a man of interest. Armfield pulled at his knotted cravat, nodding dramatically before he sat at a table. Running his hand over his shining pate, his shoulders slumped and his neck bent with the weight of his worries.

Haversham was an intimidating man to go up against after the years of battering his opponents in the ring. The owner had spent his time as a bare-knuckle boxer before he had the funds to open the club. Where he had acquired the funds was of great interest to Dash, as well as how Haversham used his powerful position over the highest nobility of the realm who frequented the club.

Dash glanced back at his fellow players' cards spread on the table before him. Seated to his left was a newly titled baron. Oblivious to the tension between the serious gamblers, Breville bantered on. "Did you hear that Lady Otford has run off with a footman?"

Dash ignored the young fop. With too much liquor and too much blunt to lose, Breville was a welcome pigeon to pluck for Vinson, Yardley, and Weber. All three men spent nights playing and had lost a portion of their wealth to Haversham. Dash knew exactly what else they had forfeited to Haversham.

Counting the played cards and running the probabilities of winning this hand of Vingt-et-un, Dash made the doomed gesture with a flick of his hand to keep in the play. His chances of winning this hand were less than eight per cent.

Sweat beaded on Weber's forehead and upper lip at the throw of a jack of hearts, worth ten points and most likely pushing him over the winning twenty-one. The portly gambler was reportedly one of the financial backers of the club. Weber, like the others, believed that fortune was in the next roll of the dice, the next flick of the card. Chasing the thrill that turned into a burning need that men couldn't fight kept Haversham in business.

Yardley, a contemporary of Dash's father, blinked away a right eye tic, and a very subtle smirk flashed on his lips. Dash threw back the exquisite brandy, allowing the heat to warm his innards, and waited for the play to unfold. Haversham delivered the best French wines and brandy, exquisite women, and French fare. It was all part of his plan to attract gentlemen to the less than reputable club. Haversham's boxing connection to the criminal element provided a seediness for the thrill-seeking gentlemen of the *ton*.

Yardley raised the ante, pushing them all to lose more money. Foolish Breville asked for another card, not paying the slightest attention to the cards dealt or the behavior of the fellow players. Breville didn't need to care about either. Dash remembered the days when there was no limit to money and the future shone bright. Not liking the turn of his thoughts, Dash threw his cards down and stood. It was time to leave. He had plans to attend to.

"Dash. It's taken me all night to find you. I thought you gave up this place?"

Dash winced hearing the disappointment in the familiar voice. He knew it was inevitable that Roddy would come looking for him. Dash thought he had more time before his friend attempted to save him from himself. Again.

Roddy, in his spotless, dun breeches, polished Hessians, and dark blue superfine wool jacket, epitomized the Earl of Clifton and respected statesman perfectly. His disheveled blond curls were at odds with the image of the serious man with serious responsibilities.

"You're back from playing hero?"

Roddy's head snapped back, giving Dash satisfaction that he had delivered the blow that he intended. "I've been back for months. Not that you would have noticed. You've obviously been distract-ed."

Dash had followed all the news of Roddy and knew his friend had been at his country estate for the last months. What Dash didn't need right now was to have his perceptive friend interfering. Dash had made sure his friend was shielded from the dark side of diplomacy in this snake pit. Haversham's was no place for England's upcoming and much needed honorable peer.

Roddy's brief glance took in the entire scene—Dash's enormous losses on the table, the smell of alcohol on Dash's breath, and his unkempt, unshaven, and wrinkled clothes smelling of smoke and cheap perfume. "Come home with me. It's been too damn long."

How easy it would be to leave this club to enjoy the company of one of the few good men in his life. But Dash had other business tonight.

"I'm busy, Clifton." Roddy didn't react to Dash's use of his title or the dismissal.

"But we have so much to catch up on." Roddy placed his hand on Dash's arm. "I want to hear all the news."

"News?" Dash stepped back from the contact. "I have none. You see before you 'my news.'" He spread his hands to encompass the raucous haze filled with scoundrels, rakes, and ladies who weren't ladies.

Dash wished he hadn't seen Roddy's look of pity before his friend forced his stiff upper lip and chippy voice. "Dita would like to see you. We are hosting a grand ball and you must attend."

If Perdita was a smart woman—and she was—she had no desire to ever see the likes of him again—unless Dash was tethered to a horse and being dragged through the street for public ridicule. Dita was a passionate woman who wouldn't forgive easily. He didn't want to think of Dita and her passionate nature. He had blocked out his past. It had all been an illusion where it needed to stay. And damn Roddy for hunting him down. He didn't want to remember. He was committed to forgetting and not revisiting the *what-ifs*.

Dash crossed his ankles and leaned against his chair. He had hoped that Roddy's younger sister would have been married by now with a passel of children. There would have been a line of men wanting to marry the stunning, spirited woman if she hadn't been so blasted stubborn and left to her own devices too long.

"I won't take no for an answer. You must attend Dita's debut ball. It's the first that she and I are hosting since my father's death. It would mean a great deal to us to have you attend."

After what Dash had done and had become, Roddy couldn't possibly still harbor hope that Dash and Dita had a future together.

Hadn't negotiating with the French dampened Roddy's belief in the goodness of mankind?

Her brother should be concentrating on a match with a respectable man. A man who would have to be strong and patient to handle Dita. A man with a firm manner who would protect her from her tendency to run wild. The image of a firm hand on Dita's body had blood rushing through his veins, stirring a desire he hadn't acknowledged in years. Damn Roddy again for showing up and igniting his need to speak with her. She had grown into a beautiful vivacious woman over the last three years, fulfilling the promising potential. From his many sources, he knew she remained a hellion on the brink of disaster.

Her father had provided very little supervision in his daughter's activities. He had packed Perdita off to a finishing school quickly after his wife died. The bastard's attention had been focused on his heir, to Roddy's detriment. Clifton had ignored all his responsibility, including presenting her to society when the period of mourning for his wife was finished, and then the bastard died and Dita had to mourn again.

Roddy had escaped his father by taking a position with Lord Hawkesbury in France as a special envoy to negotiate the Treaty of Amiens. What was to be a few months took over a year to negotiate a peace deal between Britain, France, Spain, and the Batavian Republic. Roddy hadn't returned with Hawkesbury and taken up his title after his father died. Roddy had lingered on the continent, avoiding all his responsibility to his sister. All the men in Dita's life had failed her. Dash, in the shadows, had done his best to keep both safe.

"Go home, Clifton." Dash didn't want any further mention of Perdita in front of these men who were indebted to Haversham.

"We'd love to have another player. Join us, Clifton. We want to hear what it was like to barter with the damn frogs." Yardley's smug smile bespoke his confidence that Roddy would do his bidding.

"Is it true what they say about French women?" Breville waggled his eyebrows.

Damn it. Why did Roddy have to show up now of all times? He and his team had plans for tonight. Dash had to get rid of him and in a way that demonstrated that Dash had no interest in pursuing their connection. Having his friend on the Continent had been helpful, but his reappearance was wrong for many reasons, especially attempting to reestablish their connection.

Dash considered starting a brawl except that Roddy would join in like their university days when they went looking for a good fight. Roddy was probably also under some misguided notion that Dash needed his help. While Roddy was learning the art of negotiation, Dash was honing his own methods of "negotiating."

Dash scanned the room, his brain spinning for a plausible solution when one of the club's "hostesses" smiled at him, her kohl-lined eyes transmitting her openness to possibilities. Dash grinned back and nodded to the stairs, which led to the upper rooms made available for a gentleman to slake all his needs. He was very familiar with the rooms.

Dash walked away from the table hoping that Roddy would follow. The brilliant scholar and diplomat showed his usual tenacity and tagged behind Dash.

"You're coming with me?" Dash hated the hopefulness in Roddy's tone, and that his friend could revive Dash's sense of decency.

"I've other plans." And as if Dash had orchestrated the entire scene in advance, the voluptuous blonde with rouged lips and cheeks stood before him.

"My lord, it's a pleasure." The woman curtsied as if meeting in a ballroom, giving him a view down her revealing gown. Dash had no reaction to the displayed flesh. It might be the liquor or the memory of an innocent woman with lithe curves and hazel eyes that changed colors with her mercurial moods. An innocent woman he would consume with his darkness. He wanted her shielded from the cruelty and violence that were part of his life.

"What a lucky girl I am tonight to have the attention of two prestigious men." She dipped another revealing curtsy to Roddy. She had been trained well to recognize titles. She was one of Haversham's favorites, and her approaching two earls was no accident.

"Let's be clear. I do not share." Dash lifted her hand to kiss. "But I don't think you'll be sorry."

"Well, it's a disappointment." The woman tittered. "Maybe another time, Lord Clifton."

"Excuse us." Roddy stepped between Dash and the prostitute, who smiled at Roddy despite his fierce stare.

"My God, I thought by now you'd be done with this sort of thing." Roddy's fair complexion grew ruddy.

"Sort of thing?" Dash snorted. "Pleasure in a woman's arms?"

"Forget this woman. Come back to the house. We can crack open a bottle. It will be like old times."

"Old times should be left where they belong—in the past. Don't come looking for me again."

"You don't have to live like… Why are you doing this?" The bewilderment in Roddy's voice affected Dash, making him want to share his secrets for a brief second with his childhood friend.

Dash shook his head. "Not everyone can achieve perfection in ascending to their title as you have done—a recognized diplomat and rising leader in Parliament."

Dash didn't only insert the knife; he twisted it. Roddy had suffered at the hands of his father, who had demanded perfection from his heir. At least Perdita was spared the criticism and abuse from her father.

"I'm not sure that I qualify for such high praise."

Dash hated the way Roddy's clear gaze darkened and his shoulders stiffened. Roddy had fought with his father for years, and Dash doubted they had ever reconciled their differences. Like Roddy, Dash never had the opportunity to tell his father what an immoral bastard he was.

Roddy bowed his head to the prostitute before his eyes met Dash. "Look for the invitation to the ball. You owe it to Dita to make an appearance."

Damn Roddy. The man never quit. Perdita wanted Dash at her ball as much as Dash wanted to attend.

Roddy pushed his way through the men gathered at the hazard table. A smiling Haversham bowed formally before speaking to Roddy. With his back to Dash, he couldn't see Roddy's reaction to Haversham. The boxer was as skilled in dealing with polite society as he was with hookers, gang members, and boxers. Dash tried to convince himself that Roddy was too smart and too experienced to be taken in. Yet Roddy in his prestigious world might be unable to imagine the level of debauchery Haversham was capable of.

"Excuse me, my fair lady. I will return shortly." Dash wasn't sure of his plan when he reached Roddy and Haversham, only that he wanted Roddy away from the viper. Before he could get through the crowd, Roddy nodded and walked away.

Dash felt the tightness in his chest ease as he watched his friend stride outside into the wet April night. Now all he had to deal with was a prostitute who he didn't want. And would report to Haversham every word spoken between him and Roddy.

And he thought the worst part of the night was the hundred he lost at the table. Now his nights would be plagued by memories of a woman who had ignited in his arms when he last touched her. A woman filled with passion for life and love. He hadn't been in polite society since he acquired his title. How could he attend her ball and sully her pristine reputation with his very non-pristine reputation? Maybe it was lucky to be dealing with another treasonous bastard tonight. Maybe it would distract him from his thoughts of a certain blonde temptress. Maybe.

Chapter Three

D ASH STAGGERED OUT of Haversham's as he did almost every night for those who watched. He performed nightly for an unknown audience hidden in the shadows. He was tired of the charade, but his country was on the brink of war, and he was committed to doing his part. Napoleon's advisors Talleyrand and Fouche excelled in building spy networks in enemy countries, and they had done a smash-up job in England. Dash had developed a counter network feeding false information to the French.

Jones, his footman, tonight clad in Beldon livery, opened the door to the waiting carriage emblazoned with the Beldon crest. "Home, my lord? Or to Miss Jamison's?" Jones, a seasoned soldier who had proved himself in the colonies, announced in a distinct and loud voice.

Dash visited the favored brothel of the peers regularly to assess which peer would divulge information in their cups or during post-coital talk. He fanned the rumor that he was the only customer that Amanda Jamison had allowed in her bed, giving him quite a cache among his fellow rakes.

It wasn't Amanda Jamison but a naked Perdita spread across the blanket in the dappled sunshine, her tumbled hair, the color of sunshine, around her shoulders screaming his name, that fueled every fantasy. A dream that was better than Amanda or any other woman he had bedded in the past years. Could he subject himself to the suffering that would come after seeing Perdita at the ball, knowing she was never to be his? He was reconciled to his life. The glimpse of what he had lost wouldn't make any difference to his lonely existence, would it?

"Home, good fellow." Dash tripped on the step and fell into the carriage, a performance worthy of George Cooke, the notable actor on Drury Street.

Dash leaned against the velvet cushions for a brief moment, pulling off his hat, and running his hands through his hair, taking time to rehash Roddy's visit. He savored the idea of attending Perdita's ball and holding her close as they danced. Remembering holding, touching Perdita kept him warm on the long cold nights. To be close to her again was a compelling and treacherous temptation. Yet if he indulged himself, he might never have the will to walk away again. The familiar rage stirring in his gut reminded him of how unfair were the decisions he had been forced to make.

He found it harder and harder to keep the burning fury for revenge when he knew there would be none. His father was dead and would never suffer.

He reached for the weapons tucked in the side compartment. His stableman and a skilled marksman maintained the carriage and the weapons. Dash had a small staff of trusted employees vetted by Rathbourne's men. He undid the buttons of his coat and tucked the pistol and the knife into his breeches and then rebuttoned his coat. His entire wardrobe was black. He found the same color clothing made the transition for night activities faster, and black made for better concealment. When he adapted his wardrobe, he had no idea that it would become his signature look as the "dark lord."

The drive to Dash's estate was a waste of time but necessary for the ruse. Last year, Haversham had grown suspicious and had his men follow Dash for weeks. It had been a cautionary tale of diligence and never underestimating the enemy.

Dash slowed his ascent up the steps to the stone mansion, fighting the need to hurry, so he could reveal himself to possible observers. The enormous estate was worthy of the title bequeathed to him. It was one of the many holdings he had inherited without income to maintain.

Dash pressed against the wall, waiting for Emmett to open the door. Rushing forward, the butler and trained soldier took his elbow to escort Dash into the house. With the doors closed, Dash shed his coat and his black cravat, then donned his loose-fitting coat with pockets sewn to hide tools of the trade and a cap to hide his face.

"The hackney is waiting at the corner," Emmett said. "Is there anything else you will need tonight, my lord?"

Rathbourne had several trustworthy hackney drivers who worked their regular runs but were available to drive for forgettable and unmentionable jobs. Exiting out the alley door, Dash was joined by Jones, who had shed his livery and became Dash's associate-bodyguard on these nightly excursions.

"Nothing, Emmett. Get some sleep. I have a feeling it is going to be a long night."

The men strode in companionable silence down the alley, not risking detection with any noise. Dash had grown comfortable with the large, taciturn man after several harrowing experiences. With no sense of humor and no breeding, Jones had become a compatriot and the closest to a friend in Dash's current life.

Dash had a good relationship with Rathbourne, but neither of them had time for relaxing when the future of the country was at stake. How Rathbourne had time for a wife and kept the deception from the woman was a question Dash wanted to put to the inscrutable man. Damn Roddy for showing up at Haversham's. His appearance had sparked all these fruitless meanderings. Dash would never be given an opportunity to explain his clandestine role to Roddy. Sharing his covert work could endanger his friend. Despite his diplomatic experience, Roddy's face showed a clear map of his feelings just like his sister. Roddy could never dissemble, threaten, or torture a detainee. Skills that Dash had mastered. When the war was over… Dash had to believe that Roddy would understand what drove him to take this path.

The hackney waited down two blocks and around a corner. They rotated the pickup regularly, not keeping to any pattern for this part of the night. Within minutes, they were on their way to the newest location of the naval offices at Somerset House, making the trip short. The Navy had moved their offices to the grand riverside rooms in the western half of the newly completed south wing.

"How did Armfield look tonight?" Jones, seated across from him, stretched his long legs to the side of Dash.

"Desperate and terrorized. Like he was about to wet himself. Haversham has begun the blackmail."

"It's good Haversham is predictable. It makes our jobs easier."

Haversham was careful in his selection of peers and when he began the slow process of undermining the lord to lay his trap for raising the owed debt. It was a tricky game to navigate. If the peer was pressed too hard and broke, he might go to the officials or take the cowardly way out by killing himself and raising questions.

Rathbourne's people had generated a list of men who had the potential for blackmail with their debts, gambling, alcohol, or perversity and had a position in the government and access to information that the French could exploit.

Armfield had made the list because he worked as a glorified clerk in the Department of the Navy. Armfield wasn't privy to classified secrets, but he had access to the naval shipyards, their schematics, and their production schedule.

The Treaty of Amiens was a ruse of sorts to allow England time to continue to build their already superior navy. If England was to win the war against Napoleon, it would be at sea. Acquiring ships by any means was the highest priority. Napoleon, a brilliant military strategist, would plan to cripple the shipyards. The heavily guarded principal royal dockyards were in Woolwich, Plymouth, and Portsmouth.

The docks in Portsmouth had undergone major renovations in preparation for the war. They were refitted—new wet and dry docks were excavated—and the docks themselves were drained using steam engines. These developments, because they sped the turnaround time for ships in the docks, put an end to the problem of the excessive number of ships requiring refitting to go into battle. Portsmouth would most likely be the focus of any espionage.

The second son of a viscount with a drinking and gambling problem was about to help Napoleon tip the scale in France's favor. Not on Dash's watch. And if his team had done it right, Armfield would deliver alternative schematics of the shipyard and production schedule tonight to Haversham's minion.

The carriage was parked under a tree, away from direct view and from anyone straggling down the street at this time of night, when Armfield exited the building. Armfield's office was on the backside of the grandiose main entrance, making their presence less conspicuous. The hand signals from a watcher, another soldier on Dash's team, confirmed that Armfield had arrived and was in the building and most likely stealing the substitute documents.

Dash didn't expect any trouble tonight. The part of the dirty business that he detested was the trade-off, watching a countryman save his reputation and hand over what he knew to be important to the sovereignty of his nation. Dash embraced Rathbourne's point of view that their work was the long game. It didn't deter Dash from wanting to get out of the carriage and pummel the traitor.

Neither man spoke as they waited. Dash spent his time imagining Perdita's reaction if he did make an appearance at her ball. Would her eyes soften in welcome? Dash snorted out loud. More likely, she'd gut punch him before kneeing him in the groin. Either reaction filled him with hope and then melancholy. He wouldn't witness either since he wasn't attending any ball. Jones might have to hold Dash back tonight from damaging Armfield's face. It was the only satisfaction he would have for a long while.

Dash distracted himself from images of stealing Perdita away from the ball and into the garden by watching each passerby. It was always surprising how busy the streets of London were in the middle of the night. No one caught his attention. Mainly common folk going about their business.

"Here he comes." Dash watched Armfield cross the street and signal to a hackney coming down the street. The hackney must have had a passenger since it didn't stop.

"At least he had enough wits not to travel in his own carriage." Jones chuckled. "But not enough to pay the driver to wait for him."

Armfield stood on the corner, drawing attention with his expensive wardrobe in this working-class neighborhood near the Tower of London. God, the man was a dunderhead. A massive street thug approached Armfield and grabbed the elegantly clad gentleman's arm to spin him around and punch him in the face.

Dash was first to jump out of the carriage and run to Armfield. The attacker was bent over an unmoving, prone Armfield, searching him for cash and hopefully not the papers which took hours to forge.

Instead of intervening, other men on the street changed direction, not wanting to get involved or become the next victim.

The watcher, who had been leaving the area after completing his job, sprinted toward the mugging. Dash and Jones were already moving in on the attacker who now raced away, after emptying Armfield of his belongings. They were headed toward the Tower of London and the labyrinth of alleys and streets.

"Check on Armfield," Dash shouted to the watcher as he ran. Jones, no slouch, kept pace with Dash. Was this an attack by the French or Haversham to reveal Dash's team since they were blowing their covers by chasing the thief?

Dash was fast for a big man, and his long strides caught up with the villain.

Jones was barely winded when he dove and grabbed the man by the knees, bringing them both to the ground.

"You get all the fun." Dash had pulled out his pistol and aimed at the man, watching him closely to prevent him from reaching for a weapon as Jones searched him. Dash wanted him alive to question, but if this was a suicide mission, the villain wouldn't have any trouble trying to take out Jones before succumbing.

"Hell, I done nothing wrong. A man can't go out for a walk to get away from the old lady."

The bulky man in a soiled shirt and torn breeches had rotted teeth and smelled of sweat and manure.

From his outward appearance, he was no mastermind spy. But Dash had a scar on his arm as a reminder to never to accept appearances.

"Stand up." Jones pulled the stocky man to standing, searching the front of his shirt to pull out a wad of cash.

"Look, we can split it." The man grinned, showcasing his front missing tooth.

"You think you can bargain?" Jones rolled his eyes. "Turn around."

The papers were tucked in his back pants.

"You can keep everything." He backed up with his hands in the air.

Jones handed the papers to Dash who confirmed that none were missing.

"Who hired you?" Dash asked. This should be interesting.

Confusion spread across the wrinkled, soot-covered face. "I ain't in no gang. I just need cash… Mabel at the tavern has cut me off."

Dash signaled with a head shake to Jones, who was busy binding the man's hands. The man appeared to be a common street thug with the bad luck to have picked Armfield as his pigeon.

Dash lifted his gun and pointed it at the man. "Don't try to run. I'll shoot."

Tonight was like so many others in the past three years. Shifting through the muck to find one possible pearl of information. Nothing exciting or sexy about spy work, but it sure beat the hell out of attending balls and soirees. Or did it? Both were facades but at the end of the latter, he'd have the pleasure of Perdita. Unlike tonight, when he would be alone in his empty bed with no warmth to sustain him.

"Get the cash and the papers back to Armfield. Act the part of a good Samaritan." Not that Jones needed any guidance. "And send over the watcher to take this… man back to Abchurch."

The man wasn't anyone important, but he would still be taken back to headquarters to be questioned. The buffoon had just become of interest to His Majesty's intelligence department.

Dash, pulling his cap down, headed to the hackney to wait and see whether Armfield would take the papers tonight or not. It complicated the operation if Armfield was too shaken to finish the job. Dash and his team would have to watch Armfield until he did.

Climbing into the hackney, Dash leaned against the squabs, closed his eyes, and fantasized about having Perdita waiting for him in his bed.

Chapter Four

DASH HALTED MIDSTEP at the entrance to the ballroom, employing every curse word known in the Anglo-Saxon vocabulary. Roddy and Dita were still greeting guests. There was no way to escape with Roddy beaming at him. He had timed his late arrival to avoid this precise situation. Hosts were supposed to be mingling and dancing at this time of night, not still in the receiving line.

The woman who would never be his stood between Roddy and Lady Beaumont, welcoming guests. Dash's favorite four-letter word echoed loudly as heads turned and stared at him. He looked straight ahead as he waited to greet the hosts.

Roddy knew damn well what he was asking by his invitation. Dash allowed himself to be swayed by friendship. Hobnobbing at balls and soirees wasn't a requirement of an earl. Loyalty and other emotions he wasn't willing to put a name to had driven him to make an appearance.

Dita hadn't noticed his entry. She was busy talking with Breville, the pup from Haversham's. Why wasn't she dancing? It was way past midnight. She should be busy partnering with all the eligible gentlemen worthy of an earl's sister.

There was time for Dash to make his escape, but he couldn't make himself move. Unable to look away from the animated, confident woman, he was captivated by her obvious joy. Her hands gestured as she spoke with enthusiasm, her eyes sparkled, her pink lips were parted in delight. The enormous amount of brandy he had imbibed didn't dull the blow to his chest at the sight of her.

The sheer pleasure of being close to her goodness was awful and wonderful. All the candles in the ballroom weren't as bright as her glow. She was laughing, her head thrown back in enjoyment at something said by another admiring swain.

What a fool he had been to believe he could see her and remain unaffected. He tried never to lie to himself. He didn't indulge in self-pity. He was a realist. He had done what was necessary. But tonight made him question every moment of his life. If he had trusted her with the truth, what would his life be like?

"Beldon, hadn't expected to see you here." Dash didn't think the night could get worse until Yardley projected in his parliamentary voice across the room. "This is a first. Your tastes are usually more..."

Dita's head snapped up. Shock then dismay flashed across her face when she spotted Dash. She quickly schooled herself into composure. She'd never before been able to mask her feelings or hide her reactions from him. Her face never rested in repose. She was always in motion, her mind and body spinning with energy. She had learned to protect herself from men like him. Another sin to be laid at his feet. One of many.

Time slowed as he waited for the moment when her eyes met his. The force of the connection disrupted the air around him, sending charges of shimmering brilliancy throughout the space. The candles dimmed and the music faded. His heart accelerated as every sinew tightened. She took a quick breath before she dismissed him with a flutter of her long eyelashes. Turning her attention to her next admirer, she greeted a young fop whom Dash didn't recognize.

An awful brew of possessiveness and jealousy stirred in him.

Her dismissal forced feelings that had remained long dormant. He wasn't one of the youthful suitors hanging on her smiles and sparkling eyes. He wasn't a man to be ignored. He was a dangerous man.

"My God, old man, glad you dragged yourself out of that hell-hole." Roddy shook Dash's hand.

Dash paid little attention to the exchange with Roddy. He was aware only of Dita's nearness. Her scent of vanilla overwhelmed his senses, taking him back in time. When she had asked his opinion of her perfume, he had joked that men didn't want women who smelled like a kitchen. He had lied. The scent was more potent than any exotic, sophisticated French perfume. The homey fragrance was laced with memories of golden days of laughter free from responsibility and an impending war.

She turned toward Roddy and made no attempt to lower her voice. "I don't remember Beldon being on the guest list?"

He had to suppress his laughter. She believed she could embarrass him. Crashing a ball was an ignoble deed in her world. Not in his. He wasn't the man she remembered. She assumed he would play by polite society rules. Perdita had no idea what he was capable of in service to his country. And he hoped to God she never would.

Despite her airs of sophistication, she still didn't have the sense to walk away from a challenge. She was too innocent or naïve not to realize that she had just thrown down a gauntlet that no red-blooded male could refuse. As if she had the power to assign him to society's dungeons. By his title, he would be accepted no matter how odious or criminal his activities. The presence of Yardley tonight proved his point.

She wouldn't look at him when he crowded her space, moving

close enough to see the green and golden flecks in her eyes and the blush staining her cheeks. Dita had the mouth of a highly paid courtesan with a dark beauty mark over her full pink lips. How many men had tasted those lips? Blistering hunger and lust were fomenting beneath his skin. The carnal images of what he wanted made him restless and irritable, proving what he already knew. He should not have come.

"Lady Perdita, charming as always." He lifted her hand and turned over the palm to press a kiss through her gloves. The slight tremor of her delicate wrist provided primitive gratification that she wasn't as immune as she pretended. Her skin flushed and the pulse in her throat quivered. He wanted to press his lips to the beating heartbeat and trace the path downward.

"You presumptuous ass." She pulled her hand away. Her hazel eyes flashed thunderous like gathering storm clouds. "Go away."

"Not until I have the dance Roddy promised me."

Her plush lips curved ever so slightly. It took all his restraint not to lean close and press his lips against hers to consume and absorb her amusement.

"I'm sure you'll make our ball the talk of the Season if you dance with Roddy."

"This feels like old times with you two at odds." Roddy clapped his hand on Dash's shoulder, trying to lessen the tension. "You're garnering a lot of attention. You might want to make nice." Roddy grinned widely at the guests who mingled close, not wanting to miss every word exchanged by the *dark lord.*

Damn it, he didn't come to embarrass Roddy or Perdita. Everything he said or did tonight would be the topic of conversation in tomorrow's drawing rooms. He was a master of control, but the sight of Perdita stirred everything best left in the past.

"Lady Beaumont, have you had the pleasure of an acquaintance with the Earl of Beldon?" Perdita smiled widely, displaying all her perfect teeth, and nodded to the guests who openly pressed closer. Her jaw was clenched as well as her hands at her sides.

Lord Rathbourne's aunt was a feisty good sort and had always been welcoming upon his visits to Rathbourne House.

"My lady and I are closely acquainted." Dash pressed a kiss to Lady Beaumont's palm and gave his most sensuous smile.

Lady Beaumont chortled aloud. "You rascal, Beldon. I'm sure there are many impressionable women who will fall under the spell of your charm tonight. I'm not one of them, and it seems neither is Lady Perdita." She winked at him. "I think you're going to have to work on your charm with the more discerning women."

Perdita snorted. "I believe Beldon chooses his women for their lack of discernment."

Dash grinned at Perdita, watching her fight not to say more. She had always been so easy to bait and so predictable. He doubted she'd be as easily led now.

Lady Beaumont placed her hand on Perdita's arm. "My dear, you must accept Beldon's invitation. It is most unremarkable for you to dance with a family friend." Lady Beaumont lowered her voice. "I will not allow your perfect night to be marred by all the old tabbies spreading rumors that you refused to dance with the earl."

"Of course. I won't allow anything to ruin tonight."

He would take her anger and even hatred over the resignation he heard in her voice. In his empty, lonely days, he always believed that Perdita would still care for him. She wasn't the type of woman to give up on anyone. He didn't want to know if she had changed. He should leave. He hadn't come to draw attention to Perdita or himself by dancing with her. But he never could resist her, needing her to keep pushing him, to challenge him to be a better man. For the last little while, he felt more alive than he had in years.

"My lord, you do me such an honor. But alas, by your late appearance, I've only a dance open later in the night. I'm sure you have other entertainments planned for the rest of your evening."

"It will be my honor to be granted any dance, Lady Perdita." Dash bowed. Going against all better judgment, he would stay and dance. One last look at a life he might have had.

Perdita rolled her eyes and muttered something under her breath which Lady Beaumont must have heard since she chuckled.

"It is time for us to dance together, Roddy." Perdita linked her arm with Roddy's. "Aunt Euphemia, since Beldon has a close acquaintance with you, he can escort you to your friends and attain punch and a plate. You've been standing far too long."

Knowing Perdita, Roddy was going to get an earful from his sister. Roddy would never betray that he hadn't promised a dance with Dash.

Lady Beaumont patted Perdita's cheek. "You're very sweet to watch over me, my dear. You must not worry. I'm fine. Tonight is your night, and my role is to take care of you."

Perdita pressed her hand against Lady Beaumont's. "I'm grateful to have you beside me. And I will be watching if you don't rest."

Memories of Perdita's comforting touch broke through Dash's glacial heart. Perdita was still loving and generous. He was the only one who had lost the right to her warmth and affection.

Dash offered his arm to Lady Beaumont. "Where would you like to be seated, my lady?"

Lady Beaumont leaned against his arm. "Thank heaven. My feet are killing me. I could never tell that to my darling Perdita, but I can't wait to sit down."

"She would understand."

"Yes. She would. She is a very compassionate and caring woman, just like her grandmother. It broke Annette's heart that her daughter had no time for her children. Perdita suffered from the selfishness of her parents. She was abandoned by her parents and, if I'm not mistaken, by a man too."

"My lady, I don't think Lady Perdita would welcome your speculation."

"Oh, don't get all lordy on me. Cordelier, my powerful nephew, has tried for years with no effect. I don't intimidate easily."

"I never believed you would."

"I intend to find her a worthy man. A man who will protect her and provide the love she deserves. After her dismal childhood, I will not fail Perdita. It is quite amazing that she still shows no restraint in loving despite disappointment and betrayal. She loves wholeheartedly, and the man who captures her heart will be a lucky man."

"I'm sure Lady Perdita will have many worthy men to choose from."

"Attempting to seduce her with flattery and smoldering looks or commanding her will not work. You should try for sincerity. A woman like Perdita values honesty over false admiration."

"My lady, you speak out of turn."

"Of course, I do. It's the benefit of achieving my age. I can say anything I please. Be warned. Lady Perdita is under my protection. And there will be consequences for anyone who harms her."

"My lady, I have no intention of harming her. I've no intention toward her at all. And you know very well the reason. I could never risk her wellbeing."

"During these dangerous times, is there a better man than yourself to protect her?" She batted at his arm. "Why do I waste my breath on men? You never listen, anyway. Go ahead and get me a plate and a brandy. None of that insufferable punch. Managing the young is exhausting, and standing in that blasted line made me ravenous. Bring me a second plate with Cook's sugar cookies."

Dismissed again. No wonder Perdita loved Lady Beaumont; they were both bossy. It was absurd to believe that Perdita was in danger in London. The woman did nothing that would warrant needing protection, attending balls and soirees and walking in Hyde Park.

And why did he feel cared for by Lady Beaumont's scold? No one had cared about him in a very long time except for Perdita and Roddy, whom he had both hurt and alienated. He didn't want their pity or understanding. It was much easier to reject their appeals than expose them to his dangerous enemies.

Chapter Five

EMMY TOOK DITA'S arm and pulled her through the throng toward the private quarters. "It is time to take a break. I will drag you if necessary if you stop or allow guests to engage in conversation." Emmy didn't play the role of the meek companion trailing behind her.

Dita nodded and smiled to her guests, ignoring Dash's name among the murmurs. "Your timing is impeccable. I am in need of the necessary."

Both women tittered. Dita was grateful for Emmy's steady arm as they dodged the guests who mingled in the hallway. She suddenly felt the heat of Dash's gaze on her back. Was he following her? It would be just like him to barge his way into her private quarters. She steeled herself not to look over her shoulder. She wouldn't give him satisfaction to know that he still had power over her.

She had been aware of his presence the entire evening—when he left the ballroom to either play cards or join her brother in the library to smoke cigars. The mounting dismay and anger that she wasn't immune to him was taking a toll on her composure. It was good to have this time to settle her emotions before she had to face him.

Emmy closed the door to Dita's private quarters. "You've done an amazing job of keeping up appearances. No one would know except for me and possibly Aunt Euphemia that you were upset.

Aunt Euphemia is quite perceptive."

Dita had struggled all night to pretend that Dash's attendance hadn't rekindled the feelings of the betrayed and helpless young woman.

"Thank you. I appreciate the rescue," Dita said over her shoulder as she hurried to the dressing room and to the chamber pot. Her maid waited to assist her.

"Rosetta, go down and have your dinner. Emmy will help me if I need anything." Dita didn't want Rosetta to hear any conversation about Dash. Her maid wouldn't share gossip with the downstairs servants, but Dita couldn't risk the chance. No one but her school friends knew anything about her romantic past with Dash. And she planned for it to remain that way.

"You don't want me to redo your hair?" Rosetta didn't hide her disapproval. The maid had grown up with Dita and, like Totty, didn't hold her opinions in. Rosetta was very skilled and miraculously was able to tame Dita's curls into a smooth knot on top of her head with a few curls near her face.

To Rosetta's dismay, Dita liked elegant, unadorned, and unrestrictive fashion with no bows or flounces. The midnight blue dress had a dusty rose ribbon at the bodice and around the hem. Her gloves and dancing slippers had been dyed to match the deep pink.

Dita had chosen a blue gown so she could wear her grandmother's sapphire as a symbol of taking the next step in her life. When Roddy had shared that Napoleon's two main advisors Talleyrand and Fouche had a major spy network in English society, including many among the titled, she had been first shocked and then outraged. She couldn't imagine the pain her grandmere had suffered losing her loved ones, her home, her friends, losing her entire way of life at the hands of her countrymen. Dita would use every skill and resource to stop the French from bringing suffering to English shores.

She was accepted in all households and free to move through the echelons of both English and French society. Her close relationship with the servants meant she also could rely on them to gather information. And her secret skill of martial arts would be very helpful if she ever found herself in a tricky situation. She might never be asked to negotiate with the French like Roddy, but she was adept at observing and understanding people. With the help of Emmy, Olivia, and Charlotte, she had concocted the plan to use her season to test whether she and her team could gather information and convince Lord Rathbourne to allow them to open a school for women spies.

Dita flopped on the settee and raised her feet on the table, placing them next to the tray that Totty had filled with treats. There wasn't time to untie her dancing slippers. Her legs and feet ached from the hours of standing and from clumsy partners who smashed her toes.

"Your performance was to be admired. No one would have known that you were in turmoil. You're going to make an amazing spy."

"That is very generous of you. You didn't hear me announce in a loud voice that Dash hadn't been invited or when I called him a presumptuous arse?"

Loading her plate, Emmy's face shot up. "How delightful."

And for the first time since Dash's arrival, Perdita laughed earnestly, not pretending with forced smiles and polite responses. "I would expect such kindness from a vicar's daughter. I don't think Miss Danvers would think it was delightful."

Emmy took a bite of the lobster patty. "Your comments must

not have been heard since there was no mention in the ballroom. The dark lord's appearance after not being in polite society was all the conversation. I'm glad you didn't pretend and fawn but expressed your feelings."

"Calling him an arse doesn't come close." Dita had always imagined how she would behave when she saw Dash again. Cool and sophisticated, she would act indifferent as if seeing him meant nothing to her. She hadn't behaved in any way as she had hoped. She had barely been able to hide her anger or her hurt.

"It was unfair of Roddy not to warn you."

"He was very apologetic for forgetting to mention he invited Dash. A small detail according to him. The message being that he is too busy in his work to be concerned about my social life."

"Your brother forgets nothing. He has a prodigious memory. It is why he is a brilliant diplomat."

"I'm suspicious that he is matchmaking. His success in France has gone to his head. Negotiating a truce between Dash and me would be more difficult than bargaining with Talleyrand or Napoleon himself."

"Matchmaking?" Emmy patted her lips with a napkin. She behaved more ladylike than Dita ever did. "Beldon is a rake and a gambler."

"Roddy still hopes to reform Dash. I know it has upset him to hear Dash was still gambling. There have been rumors that his estate is in the dun from his debts. My dowry would solve Dash's debt. I can imagine Roddy in his usual male conceit to believe that it's a brilliant match between his wayward sister and best friend, who are both in need of reforming."

"Your brother has no suspicions of what occurred between you in the past?"

"I've always wondered, but Roddy would have demanded Dash marry me. And I doubt Dash would share…"

"That he behaved dastardly toward his best friend's sister."

"I was a young woman weaving dreams from loneliness. He was the only person beside Roddy and Alfie who showed any interest in me. I considered myself quite mature and sophisticated. It was heady and exciting as first loves must be. I was infatuated with love. But it wasn't real. Not for me or for Dash."

She couldn't share with anyone that in Dash's arms she felt safe and needed. He was her oasis in the bleak landscape of her family. He was all that was secure and reliable. Roddy was a good egg and protected her from her father's wrath, but he had his own demons to deal with. She had survived her parents' neglect and made her own family amongst the servants and when she was sent to school. All the feelings tonight were due to nostalgia and longing for days past when she was guileless and hopeful.

But if it wasn't real, why did she feel like lightning had struck when their eyes met? Or why her skin burned, and the candles shone brighter by his near presence?

"You're blaming yourself when he is the one who behaved like a cad."

Dita never told her friends how she always regretted that Dash had stopped the kissing and touching. She had been the one always pressing herself against Dash, not knowing what she asked for, but knowing there was so much more. He was the one who'd shown restraint.

"What is it, Dita?

"I don't understand my reaction. At first I hated him, then I mourned him, and then with time all my feelings faded. But seeing him, it's as if nothing has changed. My mind knows, but my body seems to be betraying me. Is that possible?"

Emmy bent to pour tea for them as Dita stacked her plate with a few tidbits. She didn't have much time before she had to return to the ball and dance with Dash. She didn't want to be near him. She was afraid that Dash's touch could turn her into one of the silly women who lost all their dignity. She had seen many fawning, pressing against him. "I can't be like Lady Wigley rubbing herself against him."

"Or Lady Marrowstone, who announced in the ladies' retiring room that he had ruined her for any other lover. He is very virile and quite charming, despite his reputation as a dangerous man."

"You found him attractive like all the other women?"

"It is a little difficult to weave romantic fantasies when the gentleman's only interest is in prodding you with questions about your dear friend."

"He didn't? The nerve of him to use you in that manner. I will speak to him. When I saw him dancing with several of the wallflowers, I started to believe he had returned to the man I remembered."

"I wasn't sure if you or Aunt Euphemia had pressured him to dance with me."

"I would never, without consulting you first. I have great respect for Aunt Euphemia's ability to make her wishes come true, but no one can make Dash do anything he doesn't want to."

Emmy laughed. "I understand why women would want to be used by him. He is very handsome in a brutish way. When he focuses his attention on you, it is easy to understand his appeal."

"I'm not sure if you're teasing or not."

"I cannot find the man pleasing when I know how he has hurt you in an unconscionable manner. No matter how you blame yourself and believe you misunderstood. He was older and experienced and someone you trusted."

"Thank you for your defense, but I honestly know that men kiss many women and don't think of a future together. And I know you're not so naïve to believe that either. I was lonely and young and had no experience to have a perspective on a few youthful embraces."

"Well, I'm not as understanding as you are. I allowed him to make incorrect assumptions about your romantic entanglements. He is very skilled in asking questions and took great interest in your doings. There were never any direct questions about your prospects for marriage. He took the role of your brother's friend of long standing."

If Dita's feet hadn't hurt, she would have jumped up and hugged her friend. "I'm always amazed that you're a vicar's daughter. It must be all those sermons on vengeance that you had to listen to as a child."

Emmy smiled. "You might be right. There was a time when I..."

"Stop teasing. What did you do?"

"I didn't lie if that is what you're thinking. I implied you were very interested in a Frenchman. With your French heritage, you feel very passionate about this man."

"A Frenchman? And who were you thinking of when you concocted this romantic hero for me? And please tell me that you didn't use 'passionate.'"

"I might have said he stirred your passions. And I have never seen you so moved by a man before."

"I thought you read chemistry and mathematical tomes. It sounds like you've been reading too many novels. Who is this paragon that I'm in love with? Not Lord Beauvoir?" The viscount had been pursuing Dita for months. He was dashing and sophisticated, and he liked to talk about nothing else but himself.

"I never said you were in love…"

"Emmy, tell me."

"Napoleon Bonaparte is the man who stirs your passion. Am I not right?"

It took Dita a moment before she roared. She had to cover her mouth to prevent the cookie from shooting out. "I fear for anyone who tangles with you. It's exactly what Dash deserves for asking you. I've been reproaching myself for not demonstrating control over my emotions. I planned and anticipated this ball, and suddenly by my brother's machinations, the entire evening spun out of my control."

She had a family that protected her now. "I've been dreading the dance with Dash, afraid to discover my weak character. I just thought of a way to circumvent dancing that he will hate. We will promenade. It will give me a chance to engage with Lord Yardley in the presence of Beldon. I might be able to engage the gentleman in conversation about Napoleon, or his gambling debts to gauge his reactions. You must watch what he says to Lord Vinson after I leave to see if I stirred anything revealing. Lord Yardley always seems to be in Lord Vinson's presence. We might have to include him in our investigation by his close association with Lord Yardley."

She didn't mention to Emmy that by promenading she wouldn't have to be held in Dash's arms.

"Our premise that Lord Yardley's debts have forced him to questionable behavior is still not substantiated, only a possibility."

"Right now, all we have is speculation, and that his name was mentioned in the conversation between Roddy and his unknown visitor about working with the French. I could only hear snippets of what they discussed without revealing my position outside the door.

They spoke in hushed voices *and* in French."

"Lord Yardley might have been working with the French playing a part in the peace negotiations and is not a traitor."

Dita could always rely on her friend for clear deductive reasoning.

"I agree. I just see this information of their gambling debts as the first step in our data gathering."

Emmy pulled her gloves back on. "We must return to the ball."

Dita jumped from the settee. "I'm ready."

Having a scouting mission would help distract her from the anticipation and dread of being close to Dash. And what a whopper that she could almost believe… almost as believable as leprechauns and fairies dancing in the woods.

Chapter Six

DASH RESTED AGAINST the wall in a dark corner of the ballroom, ignoring the curious glances and conversation behind fans. Everyone tracked his movement, but no one dared to approach because of the scowl he shot when anyone tried. He was done with the inane conversation and the false fawning. His promise to Perdita kept him in the ballroom and nothing else. She would make him pay for forcing her to dance with him. The anticipation of engaging in battle thrummed through his body. His muscles and his heart quickened in expectation. Matching wits with Perdita was more stimulating than a naked woman waiting in his bed.

She glided into the ballroom, her glowing face wreathed in big smiles. She had rested during her withdrawal to her quarters. She had looked subdued and pale earlier. He wasn't sure if it was his presence or if someone had offended her. She smiled and conversed, but it wasn't the authentic Perdita. It didn't matter how long they had been separated; he could still read her moods.

Miss Rothsby followed several steps behind Perdita, maintaining her role as a retiring and quiet companion. It was all an act. Earlier, the smaller woman had dragged Perdita with a firm hold through the crowd. The companion wasn't impressed by his title or by him when he asked her to dance. Had Perdita told her of their past? She wasn't taken in by his attempt at flattery to gain her trust. He had gotten very little information about Perdita from the woman, but what he gained had him spinning.

He hid his feelings when Miss Rothsby disclosed that Perdita was passionate about a Frenchman. Underneath his façade, he was a fermenting mix of jealousy and regret. He desired only the best for Perdita, but the reality of another man claiming her made it hard to be generous. He already hated the man who would receive Perdita's affection.

No other woman had ever elicited tenderness, rage, and possessiveness. Being this close to her and knowing her future belonged to another was torture. He watched every one of her partners, trying to detect any attachment on Perdita's part. None seemed to have captured her attention. He owed it to her and to Roddy to make sure the Frenchman was worthy before he removed himself from her life. He had channels to find out men's secrets that Roddy would never be privy to.

He stepped out of the shadows and made his way to Perdita as the orchestra warmed its instruments for the next dance. Perdita smiled broadly at his approach. She curtsied formally, her eyes avoiding his. "My lord."

He bowed before offering his arm to escort her to the center of the room.

"Beldon, I'd ask your indulgence in sitting out this next dance. I find that I'm weary and would prefer a sedate walk around the ballroom."

Weary. What a crock. Perdita was never tired. She had the energy of a herd of highly strung Arabians. "Of course, my lady, whatever you wish." What was she up to?

Sparks glinted in her wide eyes, her cheeks pink and her smile genuine. He was totally captivated by the minx and whatever nefarious plot that she had hatched for him. "Let me take you to the refreshment table where you can fortify yourself for the rest of the night."

"Thank you for your kindness." Her truly unique eyes picked up the blue tones in her dress. The ever-changing shades reflected her moods—a barometer of her feelings. Tonight, the greenish blue matched the sparkle and depths of her sapphire necklace. He hated the empty politeness between them. He wanted to be in private with her and demand to know who the damn Frenchman was.

"A slow promenade would be to my liking. If I sit, then anyone can engage me in conversation. I'd prefer to choose my company." Her eyes flashed as her color heightened. Was she using him as a buffer from unwanted attention from a male admirer?

"If you're tired and would prefer to sit, I'm sure I can find another gentleman to accompany me…"

As if he would allow her to get rid of him when this was his only chance to be near her. He lifted her hand and placed it on his arm. The gentle contact flooded him with memories. Her vanilla scent wafted across his nostrils. "I'm yours to command."

She gazed at him through her lowered lashes. Distrust darkened her bright eyes as weariness spread across her face. "I need to pay my respects to Lady Amesbury and Lady Eldoret." She tried to pull her hand away, but he placed his on top. She ignored the bolt of frisson between them though he heard her sudden intake of breath.

He directed her toward the two harridans who had been ruling society since he'd left university. They had acerbic tongues and didn't spare anyone from their opinion. Perdita's revenge was to subject him to these women who wouldn't withhold their contempt despite his title. She wanted him to suffer their insults. And he would for her. He was entertained and touched that she had cared enough to seek revenge. Dealing with harpies was easy work away from his usual days.

"Lady Amesbury and Lady Eldoret." Perdita curtsied before the two dowagers. "I hope that you're enjoying the evening."

"Your ball will be the talk of the town with the appearance of Beldon." Lady Amesbury's overabundance of plumes waved in regal air as she lifted her plump chin. The woman's chest was covered in enough diamonds and rubies to float the cost of the royal navy for months.

Would Perdita reveal that he hadn't been invited, making him open to more censure?

"I'm glad to see you've finally decided to take your place in society. It is three years since you became Beldon." Lady Eldoret clicked her false teeth in disapproval. The overbite gave her the look of a ferret with her tiny, beady eyes. "I'm glad that your father will never know how you've ignored his legacy. *He* saw to his duty."

Perdita stiffened next to him.

"I'm sure he would find my lack of society appalling. He was a most social man."

"That he was. But he saw to his responsibilities." Lady Amesbury's rheumy brown eyes the color of mud focused on him.

"I'm so disappointed your nephew was unable to attend tonight, my lady. I was looking forward to a discourse with him, knowing how he holds Napoleon in high regard." Perdita smiled graciously at Lady Amesbury. "We are all holding our breath, aren't we? Unsure whether we will go to war or if the consulate will honor his promise in the treaty. I know I'm not the only one would like to hear your nephew's insight into Napoleon."

"My nephew is one the most foolish men of the younger generation. He knows nothing of what he speaks."

"Your nephew will be considered a traitor if he keeps spouting such poppycock. He's as dull as your husband's brother. We are fortunate to have men like Clifton. Unlike Amesbury or others"—Lady Eldoret lifted her lorgnette to look at Dash with great dramatic pause—"your brother reflects all that is good in our gentlemen, and why we will prevail over the French upstart."

"Admirable." Lady Amesbury's face mottled and her voice was strangled, having not recovered from the conversation concerning her nephew.

"Lady Amesbury and Lady Eldoret, may I escort you to the refreshment table or find seating for you?" Dash looked between the two women. "The hour grows late."

"We have had enough refreshments for one evening with two balls." Lady Eldoret's plume undulated as she shook her head.

"Thank you for gracing us with your presence when you have so many social engagements," Perdita added.

"The demands are taxing…" Lady Amesbury regained her hauteur and her glacial aspect.

Dash bowed his head, and Perdita curtsied before he steered her away. Why had she rescued him from the old harpies going on about responsibility? One small part of him would enjoy seeing their faces if he told them the truth about his honorable father and the depths of cruelty he inflicted when he was being social. This was one reason he withdrew from the hypocrisy of society. It seemed that tonight he was to be plagued with all the emotions he thought he had buried in the past.

Perdita looked up at him as they moved toward the far wall away from the dowagers. "I have not spoken with Lord Vinson or Lord Yardley yet."

Perdita expected the dowagers to disapprove of him, but what punishment could come of speaking with Vinson or Yardley? He could not fathom her purpose in seeking out his father's cronies.

Dash was surprised that Vinson and Yardley remained at the ball. Neither man spent much of their time at social outings, but rather brothels or gambling dens. They didn't bother with the approval of society. They were both of old titles and wielded their power in Parliament. Both of them separately spoke intensely with Roddy earlier in the evening, which was of interest. Was it about the French treaty or something more?

Dash ignored the stares and low murmured voices that whispered loud enough to be heard as they walked across the ballroom.

He is here tonight in search of a bride.

Another voice not to be outdone. *He needs her dowry, or he wouldn't marry a spinster. He's in dun territory.*

It took all his self-control not to confront the lowly snake of a woman who dared to speak of Perdita. He expected to have the worst said about him, but he hadn't foreseen that it would be assumed he was seeking a wife. And that Perdita would be his choice because of her generous dowry.

Perdita beamed at the guests, seemingly unaffected by the whispers. She had to have heard them.

"Lord Vinson and Lord Yardley." Perdita curtsied. "Just the gentlemen I had hoped to converse with tonight. How fortuitous that you have remained. I require a diversion away from polite discourse. I had hoped that Lord Sidmouth would be able to attend. He had reassured Roddy that he would. But I'm sure his responsibilities weigh heavily on him."

"Sidmouth? Why would you seek him out? He is a bore and would not liven the dancing nor discussion." Yardley waved his finely manicured hand in the air.

"I've never had the privilege to speak with our prime minister.

He is the hero of the hour, isn't he, by achieving the peace treaty?"

"His popularity will wane when we go to war," Yardley pronounced. "And all his peacemaking speeches will look as ridiculous as the man who delivered them."

Dash didn't remember hearing of any public rancor between Yardley and Sidmouth. Either drink or jealousy of the prime minister's popularity drove Yardley's rancor. Yardley was aware that the peace treaty was a ploy to give England time to build their navy.

"War is inevitable, then, my lord? Do you have inside information that none of us are privy to?"

The fine hairs on Dash's neck bristled with Perdita's seemingly innocent question. Did she have any idea what she was wading into? She couldn't possibly know of Yardley's involvement with the French. Could she? Is this what Aunt Euphemia alluded to about Dash protecting Perdita?

"Yardley, you're impertinent. Lady Perdita doesn't need to hear about the inner political fighting of Parliament," Vinson interjected to stop further discussion.

"But I do want to hear, Lord Vinson. I'm very interested in what such esteemed men as yourselves think the motive might be for Napoleon's promise of peace. We are using it to fortify our defenses. Napoleon must be utilizing the same strategy. Do you have any insight into what his ulterior motives are for the consulate to seek peace? My understanding is that he doesn't compromise."

"Is this what young women are interested in now?" Yardley's bloodshot sunken eyes inspected Perdita's form in a manner that had Dash ready to smash his fist into the hanging jowls.

Perdita laughed charmingly at the old lecher. "Even women tire of endless discussion of the weather. How many times can we discuss whether it will rain? Is it not appropriate to ask the men who make the decisions in our government whether the peace will stand or we will go to war? Women share the same worry as men for the safety of their loved ones and our country."

The bastard leered at Perdita's luminescent skin and her revealing decolletage. Dash couldn't call Yardley out. He had other plans for his lordship.

"What has happened to flirting behind fans and seduction in the garden? You're with a man infamous for seduction, and you want to discuss politics?" Yardley chuckled. "Maybe your reputation is exaggerated, Beldon."

Dash took a slow easy breath, glaring at Yardley. He didn't know what game Yardley played, but he refused to be baited. "You owe Lady Perdita an apology now."

"I see no reason…"

Dash kept his focus on Yardley's face. Had he underestimated Yardley's desperation? Or was it a brilliant move by the slimy bastard of manipulating an enemy to get Dash to react? Did Yardley suspect Dash and the information he had on the "respected peer" and wanted a way to embroil Dash in a scandal to lessen Dash's credibility?

"He's right, Yardley. I'm sure you didn't mean to offend Lady Perdita or her brother."

Yardley smirked. The same smarmy way when he had a winning hand. "My lady, I never meant any offense. I assumed too much. Please accept my deepest apologies."

"It is always interesting to hear men's perspectives. So very different from women's limited world view." The hauteur in her voice matched Lady Eldoret's at her worst. "Enjoy the rest of your evening, my lords." Perdita nodded to Vinson and Yardley and walked away with her spine straight and her chin raised.

Perdita had done a magnificent job without a threat of a duel. He rushed to catch her as she moved through the crowd. Why was she asking Yardley and Vinson about the French? He needed to warn her off. But warning Perdita, if not done with the greatest of care, would only push her to do the opposite. The only problem: This wasn't one of her escapades.

He gently took her elbow. She stopped and allowed him to place her hand on his arm. "Your skills are worthy of Lady Eldoret."

"High praise, indeed. If you spent time with ladies, you would know that it is a practiced skill to be always polite even as you deliver a set-down."

Dash led her outdoors away from the windows and crowded ballroom. He didn't want to draw attention to Perdita's reaction when he took her to task about her conversation with Yardley. He couldn't take a risk of her not understanding the danger. He knew from experience that her response would be loud and unladylike. "What was your real purpose in speaking with Yardley and Vinson? Your need to speak to the old biddies I can understand. But those old roues are not men to involve in one of your schemes. They are unscrupulous and dangerous. They won't like you sticking your pretty nose in their business." He waited, knowing she was considering kneeing him in the groin or shutting him out with a lift of her chin and glacial hauteur.

She stopped midway across the extensive space filled with urns of overflowing scented flowers and lanterns reflecting silhouettes on the stones before he could get her away from the milling guests. With her hands on her hips, she glared at him. "How ridiculous and condescending. My pretty nose? How about my brain wanting answers about the impending war? Are all women to be denied any knowledge of England's plans for war? And how it might affect our loved ones?"

Her loved ones. Roddy had traveled to France, but he was safely in England. Were her inquiries due to the beloved Frenchman? Was he the loved one she was worried about? Rage and pain, a familiar mélange of emotions, battled in Dash. He was comfortable with rage. Rage blocked out the hurt. He wanted all her worry, her affection, and love for him. And only him. Why was he always the one to be denied?

He grabbed her arm, not too gently leading her into a darkened corner, away from prying eyes. "I would never want you to be denied anything." And he meant every word except...

"Let's not argue." He didn't want to waste the private moments. They had to last a lifetime. "I've had my fill of polite discourse for one night. Unless of course, I'm to endure more unpleasant company as part of my punishment you've decided upon."

"Punishment?" Perdita's indignation sent a flash of heat and happiness blazing through him. The sparks flashing in her eyes and her complete focus on him were everything essential to his being.

"I think you have an exaggerated idea of your importance, my lord." Concentrating on putting him in his place, she didn't notice that he had orchestrated their position away from everyone. They were alone, sheltered against the house wall.

"Perdita, don't play these games with me. We used to be friends." He pressed closer, invading her space. He was unable to resist the pull to have her near.

"Used to be. As in past tense." Perdita raised her chin and stared over his shoulder. Not meeting his eyes.

"But it doesn't mean the memories are erased. The memories of you... of us have sustained me these past years."

Her head jerked up as she examined his face and measured his words.

"You think I will believe the lies and promises that you are skilled at weaving? And you accuse me of playing games. I'm not that naïve and innocent woman any longer."

His control was barely on a thread with her nearness, her scent filling his nose, and finally having her undivided attention. His control further slipped into dangerous territory when her words finally registered. Betrayal hit him like a fist to his gut. He was the man who introduced her to sensuality. And Perdita was always an eager and responsive pupil to any new challenge. The idea that she had cared enough about another man to share herself ripped apart his deep, scarred wounds.

"You allowed that pompous ass Beauvoir to… touch you?" His anger and pain came out brutish and loud. He couldn't think about Perdita naked in that man's arms. "Are you betrothed, then?"

Shock registered across her face before it was replaced with fury.

"You dare to ask me… you… with your reputation?" Her voice pitched high. Her blonde curls bounced, and by her vehement head shake, a tendril fell from the topknot down her delicate neck. Her unruly hair, like its owner, would never be contained. He wanted to feel the gossamer silk between his fingers, to bring it to his lips, and inhale the familiar vanilla scent.

"Is this another challenge? Shall we compare the numbers of our lovers?" She pushed at his chest. "I concede. Does that make your male vanity better? I can't compete with a man whose reputation is infamous."

Pain congealed into a ball of misery in his chest. He wanted to kiss and punish her for betraying their pristine love. The idea that Perdita no longer loved him opened a bottomless pit of emptiness. Fear of his bleak future overwhelmed him. The long, lonely nights spanned ahead with no relief.

He gripped her arms to shake her for destroying the one good thing in his existence. But touching her warm skin vanquished his despair. No other woman stirred him, made him forget everything but her. All the other men that had touched Perdita faded into the background. She was his center, his tether to the sun, and he would do anything and everything to regain his place. A few moments with her and the years of discipline vanished. He had to resist, but her warmth, her scent, her nearness was playing havoc with his self-restraint.

"No other man can stir your passion like me." His desperate rough voice was barely recognizable. "We're combustible together. Don't lie to me or yourself right now. You feel the fire burning between us, don't you? My body knows yours as yours knows mine."

She didn't struggle or resist his hold on her. Perdita never backed away from the truth or a challenge. It was one of the many reasons he loved her.

"This is some sort of joke between you and your dissolute chums? A bet on whether you can seduce the 'catch of the Season'? Improve your standing amongst rakes? How much do you stand to win?" Her dispassionate tone shredded his hope. She no longer believed him worth redemption.

"My God, what kind of man do you think I am? I would never share one single moment of our love. You've always been and always will be the only woman for me."

"Of all the ridiculous lies out of your mouth, this is the whopper. You were safe to explore first love… but I'm no longer that girl. And you were never the man… never mind. There is nothing good that can come of this conversation. As I said, you and I are in the past. And I plan to keep you there."

She pulled away, but he couldn't let her widen the distance. He couldn't stop touching her now that he had her near. "I never lied to you, Perdita. I meant every word I said. I was stupid and full of shame and have regretted my choice every day since."

"You were lying then, when you told me that men made promises in passion that they never planned to keep? It has been very instructional for my dealings with other gentlemen."

This evening with Perdita wasn't going like anything he had hoped or planned. Perdita speaking as if he was one of many gentlemen who released every primitive male need for his mate.

"If you're an expert on men's passions, then this won't be a problem for you."

He pulled her against him and took her lips to punish her, to demonstrate his dominance, to prove the desire between them. He wanted her surrender. But he was lost by the mere touch of her soft, warm lips. The taste of Perdita was familiar and gut-wrenchingly new.

He couldn't stop the deep moan or desperate hunger overtaking him when she pressed her lips against his, not stepping away from the challenge.

He softened to her demanding kiss, allowing her to take the lead. He felt her hesitation and the hitch in her breath when he met her aggression with tenderness. He gently kissed her, pouring in all his love, his need for her. She melted against him, wrapping her arms around his neck. Her surrender was his undoing. She belonged to him. His body rejoiced in her lush womanly contours against his hardness. He was unaware of anything but Perdita as he traced her lips, seeking entrance to her moist heat, ready to plunge his tongue into her mouth to taste her.

"Darling, meet me after the ball. I want a chance to make it right between us. I never meant to hurt you."

She stiffened against him, ready to pull away. She might not be ready for words between them but her desire, how she softened against him, and how she grasped his lapels and pulled his lips to hers, to explore with her tongue, was enough for now.

"No promises, Dash. Just kiss me."

He couldn't keep her away from the ball much longer. He had to stop, or he'd be taking her against the wall. But it was always like this with Perdita: One touch and they both went up in flames. He showered kisses on her lips, her cheeks, her forehead, not wanting the interlude to stop. But he would never bring scandal to Perdita.

He immediately released Perdita and stepped away at the sound of loud coughing and then a woman's voice. "I feel a chill coming on." The voice pitched loudly for all nearby guests to hear. "I think we must return to the ballroom, don't you, Lady Perdita? You and I have been out here too long."

Perdita startled and then jumped back against the nearby shrubs. "Oh, my God." She muttered under her breath.

Miss Rothsby moved close and whispered, "Dita, you must return to the ball. People are asking questions. Take my arm and smile."

Perdita nodded, then patted at the curls that had loosened. She didn't meet his eyes but smoothed her skirt. "Please do not follow me."

"Yes, it would be best if you remained outside for a reasonable period of time. Dita doesn't need her name linked with yours."

He was left alone in the darkness. A familiar place.

Chapter Seven

DITA SLOWLY CLIMBED the marble stairs. Attending the theater hadn't distracted her from her swirling mind or emotions and her self-disgust. What had happened to the woman who swore to never speak with Dash again?

"Are you feeling well? You were quiet the entire trip from the theater." Emmy stopped on one of the steps on their ascent to their rooms. "These late hours are taking a toll on you."

Dita was exhausted but too tired to sleep. She needed a bout of stick fighting or an early gallop on Rotten Row. Sitting in a theater box, making frivolous conversation about nothing was tiring. The Season already grew tedious, and it was only a month into activities. Her unrest had nothing to do with Dash, or that she continued to think of him and the way he could summon her feelings with a simple touch. He hadn't sent flowers the next day after the ball as many of the gentlemen had but had sent an enormous box of licorice, her favorite childhood treat.

His note in his barely legible scrawl signed with Beldon was brief and proper for anyone to read: *Sweets for a sweet woman.* Their time in the garden and his note had kept her awake, remembering when he told her after bringing pleasure with his tongue that she was sweeter than any candy.

"I am tired, not from the lack of sleep but the monotony." She hated lying to her best friend but nothing would come of discussing

Dash. "I had hoped that I would have made progress with a possible interview with Lord Rathbourne or have more information to share about Lord Yardley. The only thing I've learned is that there is bad blood between Yardley and Sidmouth and no way to find out why."

"You can't help that Lord Yardley is a bore. You can approach Lord Vinson or possibly Lord Sidmouth at tomorrow night's ball. Both gentlemen might be amenable to talking with you."

"Were you able to learn anything in the retiring room tonight about either man's mistresses?"

Emmy spent time in the retiring room listening to the other companions and ladies' conversation. It wasn't for gossip but for information that might help them in their inquiries. But it was Emmy's ability to read lips that was their secret weapon. In her father's parish, there had been a deaf family. Emmy had helped the family to find ways to communicate with the other parishioners so the family would be less isolated from the rest of the community. And now it was part of their plan to teach how to read lips for intelligence gathering. The technique had its draw back since you had to have a perfect view of the subject, which could be tricky in a crowded ballroom. And it wasn't completely reliable.

"Nothing in the retiring room tonight except that Lady Yardley detests her husband and spent little time in his company. It isn't surprising that he spends his nights at Haversham's gambling club."

"I've been a fool to believe the gentleman would speak with me about anything of substance. You, Totty, Rosetta, the footmen, and stablemen aren't bound by social proprieties and are able to ask questions. Whereas I'm treated as if I'm some sort of social misfit. I don't know how I will endure the Season without contributing anything." And not have a distraction from thinking of Dash. "If we aren't able to have our school, you'll still have your studies, Olivia will pursue her mesmerism, and Charlotte might take to the stage. All I will have is a very busy social calendar and constant pressure to marry from Roddy and the *ton*."

"You are tired. This is not the Dita I know. Seeing Beldon is weighing on you. And you're pressuring yourself too much about finding more substantial information for Lord Rathbourne. Tomorrow will look better. Rome wasn't built in a day."

She smiled at Emmy with the shared memory of one of Miss Danvers's adages.

Emmy was correct that Dash was constantly on her mind. But her friend had no idea that her prank had unleashed Dash's need to prove that the Frenchman hadn't won her heart. And like a fool, she had kissed Dash, trying to prove she was unmoved. She was always a sucker for challenges of any sort. Dash used his knowledge against her. She wanted to rage, but she could only fault herself for letting the need to win expose her vulnerability. She was no wiser or experienced in understanding her needs or Dash. In his arms, she had returned to being the naïve young woman who believed his touches and kisses meant something more than a game. She wanted to understand his reason for leaving her, but she didn't want to relive the miserable months of heartbreak. She had too much to lose to renew contests with the rake.

"We have to find out the reason why Lord Yardley makes visits to the docks. If we are to accept what his stableman has reported to Harry about the lord's activity, Yardley might be involved in smuggling, which would be a scandal but not something to take to Lord Rathbourne. I think it might be worth having Harry, our stableman, follow Lord Yardley once Alfie leaves for Sussex."

Alfie took his role as Dita's protector very seriously and would never approve of Dita playing an active part in gathering information or involving Dita's childhood friend and his assistant in clandestine activities. She hadn't yet shared her idea with Alfie that she personally would be gathering information. She had a pretty good notion of how Alfie would react.

"Is it a possibility there is a link with Yardley's gambling debts to Haversham and his trips to the docks?" Dita and Emmy often discussed every avenue of information and how it related to possible espionage.

"Maybe we should be looking more closely at Haversham. Lady Billingsworth wasn't discreet in her conversation with Mrs. Donaldson about the club owner. The Duke of Leicester has never acknowledged his bastard son. They were quite titillated that Haversham was a bare-knuckle boxer and is associated with criminal elements. They said it was the makings of a Gothic novel. It is amazing what we've learned by paying attention at the social events." Emmy laughed.

"I wish we had a way to gain information about the workings of the club. Haversham is most likely involved with smuggling of liquor and maybe he has ties to the French. But why would Lord Yardley be involved with smuggling? To pay off his debts to Haversham? We need someone in the club."

"Charlotte could probably carry off going in disguise," Emmy added. "You would be recognized, and I would never have the courage to try."

"Many of the men of the *ton* spend their late nights there." Dita wasn't used to fits of self-pity, but thinking of how Dash spent the last years reinforced how little experience she had in understanding men's needs. She had believed that he loved her as much as she did him. But no longer did she harbor such childish fantasies. Her parents' marriage was a cautionary tale if there ever was one.

"Come on, I'll have Rosetta heat a cup of milk for you."

"I will retire soon, but I am in need of something to read." She would never admit that she needed a book to distract her from another night of remembering Dash and how she melted against him and hadn't wanted to stop. The daytime kept her busy and unable to dwell on useless thoughts.

Dita strode down the hall to the library. She would find a Gothic novel to get lost in with its gruesome details.

"Billy, you may retire. There is no need for you to remain at your post," Dita addressed the young, gangly footman, who was quite proud of his new elevation from boot boy to footman.

"My lady, his lordship may need me."

"My brother is home?" Dita hadn't seen Roddy since the ball two nights ago.

Billy opened the door for Dita to enter. A fire roared and all the candles were lit. Roddy, with his shirt sleeves rolled to his elbows, sat behind his desk, which was covered in stacks of papers. A snifter of brandy was within his reach.

"Roddy, I didn't think I'd find you home. It seems that you are never in residence."

He ran his hand through his messy, thick blond curls. They both shared their father's tall, lean stature and curls that refused to be tamed. Tall stature wasn't as prized for a woman as for a man. She had endured both Roddy and Dash calling her bean pole or stretch when she was growing up.

"Not any more than you. Your calendar is quite full. How was the theater?"

Dita flopped on the couch in front of the fire. Stuffing a pillow behind her head, she propped her legs on the arm of the settee. "Boring. Everything you would expect from sitting in a box for hours with nothing of substance discussed."

Roddy brought his snifter of brandy and sat across from her, stretching his long legs in front of the hearth. "That bad? But you always enjoy the company of people and find good humor in any situation. Maybe you are still tired from the ball? Organizing such a grand fete was demanding."

"You might be right."

"You *are* out of sorts to concede so easily that I'm right," Roddy teased.

Dita laughed. "Mathematically speaking, there have to be times when you're correct."

"How generous you are, Dita. If you continue in this manner, I might not recognize you."

"Do you have any news of the war that you can share?"

Roddy rarely shared and was very adept at changing the topic. "We discussed the production of battle ships and recruitment to man the new ships. Taking men from the farms and their trades has implications for our lands and future food shortages."

Dita hid her surprise that Roddy willingly discussed his meetings. He must be tired. "Thank you. I appreciate when you can give me insight into what our country faces."

"You are the most curious woman I know… but I would think you have more interesting news."

Dita turned her head to inspect Roddy's face. Had Roddy heard about Dash and her on the balcony? They hadn't exactly been discreet. Or possibly, Yardley or Vinson mentioned her questions.

"Nothing of import." Dita smiled.

"There are bets at my club about a Frenchman who has captured your attention. The betting is heavy. Lord Beauvoir is favored to become your betrothed."

Dita jumped off the couch, feeling a sudden burst of energy. "It was a joke. I can't believe that the rumors have spread so quickly."

"A joke? I don't understand. Has Beauvoir won your affections? I know he has shown interest."

"No. Never. The man has only one topic. Himself." Dita paced in front of the fireplace. "Emmy commented that a Frenchman stirred my passions to distract all the questions about my possible suitors."

He saw it as his responsibility to find her a suitor. She couldn't burden him with her lack of interest in marriage when he had so many responsibilities.

"I'm relieved to hear he is not the one you've chosen. I find him insufferable."

Roddy and Perdita laughed together. And for a brief moment, all was right in her world. Memories of Roddy, ignoring her governess and taking her out for a ride when her parents were engaged in one of their screaming battles, took her out of her brooding. He had tried to shield her when he was home. She had finally made her escape when she was sent to Miss Danvers.

"I'm glad that we are in agreement." Dita sat down.

"I had always hoped that you and Dash…" Roddy stared at the fire. "I can't think of a better man for you. But now… I don't know what to think. He would have kept you in line where I have failed." He looked up from the fire and grinned.

Dita couldn't take umbrage with Roddy. Not when the mood between them was warm and comforting. She had missed her brother when he had been in France. But she rarely saw him now that he returned. He was weighed down with demanding and heavy duties which he barely shared with her. He'd hoped that his work with the treaty would have prevented the war commencing.

"Have you ever thought I might have been the one to keep Dash in line?" The comment had been said in jest but neither laughed. There was an unspoken agreement shared when their eyes met.

"You would be the best antidote for what ails him. You're the light to his darkness. You could always make him laugh, take him out of his black moods."

"His need to gamble? Some say it's an ailment that people can't control. Does he have the sickness? I don't think there is a cure."

"He never had any trouble when we were young bucks on the town. He was always bored since he always won with his genius mathematical skills. Some gentlemen get in deep quickly, but Dash was always able to walk away from the game."

It seemed Dash was a master of walking away from many things.

"When his father died, I'd thought he'd be happy that he didn't have to deal with the cruel man."

Dash had never shared what he had suffered under his father's hand, but Roddy had. Dash's father was worse than theirs. Which in her mind had to be pretty awful. Roddy would never give her any details except that Dash's father had an explosive temper when he was in his cups, which was often.

"I never understood why he withdrew completely from polite society and his friends." *And me*, she wanted to add.

"He hated his father… and at first everyone assumed he was celebrating his new freedom before taking on the responsibilities due his rank. Except he never returned to society and kept gambling. Since I've been back from France, I've heard rumors that his estate is suffering from his gambling debts. I tried to offer my assistance, but he was adamant that he didn't need my help."

"He is too proud to admit to needing aid."

Dita and Dash were alike. They had both been forced to learn to rely on themselves at an early age.

The firelight on Roddy's face reflected the stress lines around his eyes and mouth. She hated that he carried so many burdens, and there were so few of which she could relieve him. "You're a good friend, Roddy. And Dash might not show it, but he knows he can call on you for anything. You were able to get him to attend the ball."

The door burst open as a breathless Billy, who couldn't contain his excitement, rushed into the library. "My lord, an urgent message has come for you." Billy offered a note on a silver salver.

Roddy tore the sheet open.

Tension extinguished the warm intimacy of the room. She watched Roddy's eyes track the words on the page. She held her breath. Only matters of state could be this urgent.

Roddy threw the paper into the fire and then rolled his sleeves down. "Billy, tell Reese to get my horse. I need to leave immediately."

Dita waited until Billy had gone. "What is it, Roddy? What is so important?"

"It's from Dash. He needs my help immediately. He asked me to meet him at Haversham's."

Roddy strode to his desk, opened a drawer, then pulled out his pistol. He tucked it in the front of his breeches and then slipped on his jacket, which hung on the back of his chair.

"You plan to shoot someone?" Dita sorted through all the possibilities of why Dash would need Roddy's help after rejecting any form of assistance. She rubbed her arms to fight against the icy dread filling her.

Roddy patted his hair down and grinned, looking younger suddenly. Her brother was excited for an adventure. "Of course not.

But it works to intimidate people when you brandish it confidently."

"Dash is in danger? Is that why he has summoned you?"

"Most likely he needs me to vouch for his debt. Nothing else makes sense. Men who don't receive their funds can be demanding. Don't worry. Dash can handle himself."

She swallowed against the alarm crawling up her throat, making her voice wobbly. "You'll notify me once you've returned?"

Roddy headed to the door, looking over his shoulder. "It will be late. All will be fine. You need to get some sleep."

And with a nonchalant nod of his head, he left her. Left her to worry and stew over the risks of what he and Dash might face. And like a hardened warrior, his mood had gone from tired to exhilarated by the possibility of danger.

Chapter Eight

DITA HID IN the shadows, shifting her weight from foot to foot in her ill-fitting boots. Her heart was aflutter like a caged bird thrashing against its bars. She tugged at the rough wool collar chafing her neck while balancing the large wicker basket on her arm. She panted to avoid inhaling the odiferous stench filling the alley. She would have to replace the scullery maid's boots and dress. The stains and smell of horse and human muck would never wash out.

Loud guffaws of laughter echoed down the empty street as the men poured out of Mr. Haversham's gentlemen's club in the early morning. It didn't require a robust imagination of how men of means and privilege entertained themselves through the night. She was a muddle of emotions. Fear with an undercurrent of anger for her brother and Dash, who probably were enjoying themselves in the club as she spent the last two nights awake with worry since Roddy received the urgent note. She had sent messages to Roddy's other clubs and his office in Parliament since he hadn't returned home. And the entire time she spent in concern, he was most likely back to his disgusting behavior with Dash in the club. Harry, the stableman, had told her that men spent days in the club without ever leaving.

The doors to the club had promptly opened at seven a.m. as Harry had predicted. She had been standing for over thirty minutes in the darkness waiting for this precise moment.

She scurried into the street, preventing anyone from noticing her entry from the alley. Before embarking, she pulled at the brim of the oversized bonnet. With her head down, swinging her basket, she assumed the role of a distracted maid in no hurry to get to the market. No one would consider that she, Lady Perdita Tinley, would be unaccompanied in a questionable area at such an unfashionable hour.

Lord Randolph, a friend of her father who'd always leered at her when he visited, sauntered out through the doors in a fine fettle, smiling and swirling his walking stick. The baron showed no signs of a night of dissolution or debauchery. His cravat was impeccable, his coat without a wrinkle. By his cheeky grin, he must have had a good night at the tables. Perdita shut down any other images of what else would make him look jubilant.

It took all her self-control, which wasn't at its best after standing still, not to shout out and chase after him to ask about her brother. She slowed her steps and gave herself a good talking to. The purpose of this morning was observation, not confrontation or questions. It would serve no purpose to expose her identity and be ruined in society.

She was here only to either find Roddy or identify the men who gambled at the club. She could guess at the identity of some of the wastrels. But she needed to know the men who frequented this club to ask them at tonight's ball about Roddy's absence.

There was no discreet way for a lady to discover the names of the gentlemen who spent their night at the notorious gambling club. What gentleman could deprive a blushing lady, with a title and a very substantial dowry, an answer to her queries? Rosetta as well as Emmy had demanded they wait outside the club and report back instead of Dita risking her reputation. But how would Rosetta recognize men of the *ton*? And Emmy might recognize some but not all. It had to be her. She didn't share with the women that she had to act to end the helpless feelings. Waiting and worrying for both Roddy and Dash had pushed her to her limits of coping.

She slowed her steps to not bump into another of her brother's wild friends, Lord Tumbley, a hanger on to the group of Roddy's dissolute chums from his past. Her older brother had left all his dissipated chums behind after university. He had returned to his behavior of not coming home at night, having questionable men appear at their door at all hours, a few months before he suddenly announced that he was headed to France to help negotiate a peace treaty between the warring countries.

An older, overweight gentleman stumbled out into the street. He rubbed his hooded eyes as if the gray May morning light was too bright. A chill of apprehension skittered down her spine at his close proximity. His eyes raked over her before dismissing her when he turned and was joined by Lord Yardley and Lord Vinson. She didn't recognize the fleshy man. It was rather remarkable in that she knew most all of society's gentlemen, or so she had thought. How would she be able to make her inquiries if she didn't know the gentleman?

The fear that Dash had been challenged to a duel over some ridiculous male posturing, asked Roddy to be his second, was the worst scenario and the one that logically made the most sense. She assumed there would be news by now. But none of the servants had heard any gossip, and she was left to wait. Not her strongest virtue.

She was convinced she would know in her heart if Dash was dead. The idea of the world without Dash caused primitive panic. The clawing, breathless, heart-racing feelings she kept at bay during the daylight hours now oozed beneath her skin, like dampness seeping into the soles of her boots. She was terrified and didn't know who to turn to. She had considered approaching Lord Rathbourne, but she had no information and didn't want to raise the alarm if her brother and Dash were renewing their friendship and their dissolute ways in the club. It would color Lord Rathbourne's perception of her steadiness and possibly ruin any chance of their school. But if she didn't have answers by tonight, it was her next action.

Anxiety quickened her steps until she was directly in front of the entrance. It took all her mustard not to turn her head for a glimpse of the den of sin, the infamous club that was whispered about behind fans. She was already past the club with barely a glimpse of only a few men. She had to delay her progress down the street. She had hoped to broaden her field of possible men to question. She bent, feigning that her boot lace had become untied.

How long could she remain in this position? If she had been really clever, she would have faced the entrance so she could sneak peeks of the men exiting. But wouldn't it seem strange to change direction? She twisted to look back, but the blasted rim of her bonnet prevented her from seeing anything without looking up and revealing her face.

"Now what do we have here? What a delightful vision of womanly curves to rouse a man so early in the morning." Perdita stilled, suddenly aware of the sound of the voice and footsteps moving toward her. She had remained too long.

"I never been an early riser but this morning…"

Loud guffaws followed with back slapping by the sharp sound.

Perdita stood slowly, aware of the danger, trying not to stimulate the predator's nature to chase and capture.

"I saw her first, Frankland."

Lord Frankland, the darling of the ton, was all blond curls and blue eyes. Her brother had mentioned him as a possible suitor. "I'm a patient man. I can wait for five minutes."

And for some reason that made the men break into laughter.

Fighting the alarm flashing through her, she focused on taking one step, then another and another. Keeping her focus ahead.

"Where are you going, my darling? Turn around. Let's see if the face matches up to the promise of your body."

She stiffened and kept walking. Surely, one of the other gentlemen wouldn't allow a servant to be accosted on a street.

A steely hand gripped her arm, squeezing tightly. The smell of alcohol and rank breath enveloped her. Despite his drunken state, the man's superior strength was evident. "Haven't you learned to obey your betters?"

Frankland's chuckle enflamed her righteousness. What gave these gentlemen the right to accost any woman? Especially a servant, who should be under a gentleman's protection.

His hand tightened when she tried to pull away.

With his powerful grip, her mind shifted into focus. She twisted, using her body weight to deliver a chopping blow against her assailant's forearm. Shocked by the sudden forceful attack, he released her arm. She smashed her basket into his face, recognizing her assailant as none other than Mr. Cole, another darling of society.

"Feisty, huh? It only makes the sport more satisfying."

Frankland's laughter sparked furious outrage for all vulnerable women. She rolled to the balls of her feet and took a level breath, ready to defend and strike. She would teach these fools the consequences of their insidious actions.

"Cole, you arse. Let the girl go."

Her heart plummeted to her shaky knees. She recognized the languid drawl. Not so languid, presently. She had been in love with the deep bass voice and the perfect specimen of male virility since she was eight years old. The first time Dash came to their home.

Shock had her frozen in place. Relief and rage tore through her. She had been right all along. Dash and Roddy had been in the club debauching and gambling while she had been terrified. Her better sense told her to leave, but the storm of emotions made her want to turn and scream and do bodily harm to Dash and her brother when he finally came out into the daylight.

One tiny part of her brain cautioned against an outburst. Her identity would be revealed, and she would be compromised by Frankland and Cole. And society would expect her to marry one of those craven fools or, heaven forbid, Dash with all the rumors swirling in society about them.

She waited for Dash to confront her. He would recognize her fighting style. She had to believe he would never ruin her. So, she did what only a woman of intelligence and a strong sense of self-preservation would do at this critical juncture. She lifted her skirts and ran.

Chapter Nine

DASH QUESTIONED HIS sanity in choosing a ball to confront Perdita. He hadn't wanted to betray her morning escapade to Roddy by going to Clifton house. Now he was regretting his honorable choice. Only Perdita was capable of reducing him to question his judgment. He stood with a matchmaking mama who had found him hidden in an alcove. He'd rather be hung, drawn, and quartered than endure one more moment of this faked politeness. This was all Dita's fault, and he planned to make her pay royally when and if she arrived. He wanted to wring her pretty little neck for placing him in this ridiculous situation. If he were honest, if he touched her, retribution wouldn't be on his mind.

"My lord, I hope you'll attend my musical soiree next week. Matilda and her sisters will be performing. With your absence from society, you're probably unaware of Matilda's rare talent." And the pushy mother poked her daughter with her elbow. He assumed the chit with her hands clenched together and her gaze on the floor was Matilda. He hadn't listened to the introductions as he plotted his escape and the punishment he planned to dole out to the woman who had no musical talents.

"It would be an honor, my lord, to play for you." Matilda, a mere child, blushed to her hairline when he smiled at her. He felt sympathy for the poor lass who, like him, would rather be anywhere than having this conversation.

Where was Perdita? His valet reassured him that the Billingsworth ball was the event of the evening. Had she been injured or detained by other men in this morning escapade? He shouldn't have allowed her to escape. He should have run after her and damn the consequences. He immediately recognized her graceful motions from the hours of practicing together as she delivered the blows to Cole. The woman deserved a good spanking for coming to Haversham's. Visions of Perdita's rounded derriere between his hands made it uncomfortably warm in the ballroom as the mama droned on like an irritating gnat.

Why was she taking a risk visiting Haversham's? She would be ruined if anyone learned of her pretending to be a servant and that she had been exposed to the gentleman's lowly appetites. If he hadn't been there to stop them, Frankland and Cole could have pulled her into an alley and ravished her. The idea of those men touching her, hurting her, enraged him all over again. If he hadn't wanted to protect Perdita's reputation, he would have challenged them. No gentlemen should treat Perdita or a servant in such a despicable manner. He would eventually take care of Frankland and Cole.

Upon his arrival, he quickly realized that standing near the entrance to catch the wayward hellion forced him to greet each of the sundry guests. His position in a corner hidden by a blossoming tree and the dim candlelight didn't stop Matilda's mother from cornering him. And when did he resort to hiding? Since Perdita whizzed back into his life. And he had never felt more invigorated.

"Excuse me, but I'm committed to another engagement." He strode across the room, not acknowledging the smiles and the greetings. He was done behaving the part of a gentleman. Tomorrow he would drive to Clifton house. She needed to learn the consequences of her behavior. He was wiping his hands clean of the damn woman who attracted trouble like bees to the flower. It was Roddy's responsibility to manage her. Except Roddy didn't manage her. In fact, it was the reverse. Perdita had run circles around Roddy since they were children. She had no one who guided her except the servants, who were devoted to her but held no power over her recklessness. And if someone didn't intervene, she was going to be ruined or worse… unless she married. The poor fellow would need a great deal of stamina to keep up with Perdita. Envisioning Perdita's stamina in bed had him tugging on his cravat, which seemed to have turned into a garrote. Lady Beaumont's comments about another man assuming responsibility for Perdita had plagued him as he imagined the man introducing Perdita to sensual delights. He had to exit now.

His black mood must have translated to his fellow guests since he had a clear path to the door when he heard her laugh. It was joyous and floated along the notes of the music.

At the entrance, a beaming Perdita, radiating confidence and beauty, stood with none other than the preening peacock, Beauvoir, with his carefully arranged curls falling over his brow. Black spots flashed before his eyes as he reined in his unchecked lust and anger into a barely manageable *I won't grab and throttle her or ravish her.* Every muscle tightened, his breath accelerated, and his vision focused on his prey.

Every second, every minute of the last hours that he had spent worrying about her, imagining her in another man's bed, coalesced into a ball of hot fury. She was untouched by this morning's escapade when he had been reduced to fretting like an old nanny. And more grievous was appearing at a *ton* event to maintain her reputation. His fists clenched at his side.

Perdita must have felt his fury directed at her. She stopped mid-smile and midstep. She froze like a frightened rabbit, her eyes darting to the right, looking for an escape, avoiding to meet his eyes. He glowered at her, fully aware of the power of his intimidation skills. Wanting her to feel his wrath and the consequences that awaited her. And the damn woman had the gall to glare back at him, before she lifted her chin and turned to the Frenchman who he would tear apart after he was done with her.

"Lady Perdita, I've urgent news from your cousin and need a moment of your time." The cousin she despised and thankfully rarely saw. Dash crowded between Perdita and her Frenchman. "I'm sure Beauvoir won't mind."

Beauvoir stepped back, widening the distance from Dash. Perdita was the only person who wasn't cowed by his *I'm going to rip you apart* stare.

"I'm sure whatever news you have can wait. You may call on me tomorrow to deliver the message." Her eyes narrowed as she lifted her chin again with a hauteur worthy of the old dames.

Dash was in no mood for games. Did she know how close she was to being dragged out of the ballroom? He clenched and unclenched his fists to gain control. After spending hours in the ballroom, his long-admired calm vanished. He was about to cause a scene after his attendance had been explicitly intended to avoid any scandal. He took her arm and tucked it not so gently into his. "This cannot wait."

She ground the heel of her dancing slippers into his foot as she attempted to whisper through her growls of outrage, "Unhand me or I will scream."

"If you would like to call attention to us, go ahead. I'm beyond scandal, but I think you will be the one to suffer." He bent to her ear. "Unless you want to be forced to marry me?"

"When the Thames dries up." Her exasperated sigh was strong enough to blow the feather plumes tucked into her curls before she spoke loudly to make sure the people in proximity heard every word. "I'm all ears to hear of my cousin. I hope nothing horrible has transpired."

Her green silk gown outlined her slender curves, and the tender skin above her bodice was mottled and fiery, as was her face. Magnificent in her fury, all his thoughts of retribution faded as he imagined pressing his lips to the heated flesh. She was the only woman who could distract him from his purpose. He exhaled deeply and led her through the crowd to the French doors, then outside to the balcony. It wasn't a warm evening, but many gentlemen were gathered to escape the sweltering airless ballroom. A few couples also had escaped the confines of the ballroom to dally in corners.

"You're insufferable. After the hours of worry that you and Roddy have put me through, I'm not to be dragged across the ballroom like some child."

He kept his grip on her arm as he moved away from the men on the balcony and away from anyone who could hear their conversation. He pivoted so her back was to the gentlemen. He didn't want anyone to witness her reactions. Unlike him, she was a hothead, and some buffoon might feel he had to intervene in her distress.

"Do not try to distract me. You were disguised as a servant at Haversham's this morning."

"I knew you were going to overreact, and somehow I would be found at fault."

"You talk nonsense. Of course, you're at fault. Do you know what could have happened to you?" He was back in the grip of anger and fear.

"I wouldn't have to search…" She pulled her arm away. "I assume whatever crisis was abated…"

"Do not change the topic." She was clever and quite adept at avoiding responsibility. "What feather brain idea drove you to appear at Haversham's?"

"My behavior is of no concern to you." In the dim light, he glimpsed a flash of hurt before she lifted her chin and regained that cool haughtiness that he was starting to hate. "Where is my erstwhile brother? I assume if you're here, then he is too. I have a few words for him."

"Roddy's whereabouts are not my concern. But yours are since you seem bent on the need to ruin yourself."

She snorted in a very unladylike manner, all vestiges of the grand dame gone. "Coming from a man who is known for his debauched life and nothing else, you have the nerve to speak to me about my reputation. If you're finished with the insults, I'd like to find my brother. You may have a need to destroy yourself, but I won't allow you to drag my brother into your downfall." Her voice quivered and her chest heaved.

She was genuinely upset and held him responsible for Roddy's behavior. He had been so focused on frightening her to stop her hoydenish ways, instead of pulling her into his arms and pouring out his pent-up feelings, that he hadn't listened for an explanation. What had Roddy done to warrant such a strong response? "What exactly you are accusing me of?"

She rolled her eyes upward, and her plumes danced in the midnight sky. "Since your reacquaintance with my brother, he has forgotten all his duties."

She pivoted to walk away, then turning back, she said, "Unlike Roddy, I'm not susceptible to your enticements of depravity."

He grabbed her arm. "Perdita, I have no idea what you're speaking of."

"And you talk about me trying to distract you from the matter at hand. You know exactly what I speak of. Roddy and you spending days and nights at Haversham's."

"If this is some game you're playing, you will be sorry that you started it." His anger toward Perdita was overblown and misguided. The fury was directed at himself and what an unfair hand he had been dealt. Right now, if things had been different, he would have a say in Perdita's activities, and she'd be in his bed and not have the time and energy for dangerous adventures disguised as a servant.

"I should have known you wouldn't take any responsibility for your actions. You haven't changed."

The accusation was like a kick to his solar plexus. It was the hurt and the disappointment in her voice that was his undoing. He wanted to hold her and tell her that she was the shining light on the grim path he was destined to follow. Always had been and always would be. And he regretted his actions toward her every day. He couldn't let her go on believing he didn't love her. It didn't matter that she would reject him, he wanted her to believe that she was lovable. He had convinced himself that he was protecting her by not telling her the truth about his inheritance, but he only protected himself. He had been a selfish bastard hurting the only person who had ever loved him.

"I haven't been with your brother at Haversham's. I haven't seen Roddy since your ball."

Perdita stopped and pivoted to face him. Her eyes narrowed as she searched his face for lies. Did she think so little of him? "I haven't seen him, Perdita. Is he here tonight? He will acquit me of all charges laid against me."

Her eyes widened and Perdita, who wielded acerbic words like a sharpened blade, stuttered. "But... but you sent him a note. I was with him when he received it. You said he had to meet you at Haversham's. It was urgent. He left at three a.m. two nights ago to meet you." She lost all her color and began to shiver.

He pulled his jacket off and wrapped it around her shoulders. She was truly in shock and didn't react to his ministrations, allowing him to keep his arm around her longer than needed. If they weren't already attracting attention, he would have taken her into his arms and held her. He hadn't sent Roddy any note. The instinct that he'd honed during the last few years heightened. Something foul had occurred. Possibilities of treachery and the possible perpetrators created a long list by his role in the silent war waging against France. His enemies were willing to use anyone as a pawn against him. Was his closest friend hurt because of him?

"I'm going to take you home. Is Lady Beaumont your chaperone tonight?" He didn't want the all-seeing eyes of the *ton* to witness her distress.

"Lady Beaumont had another commitment but planned to join me here as Lady Billingsworth is a dear friend. I don't know what other social engagement she could have. It was rather baffling," she rambled as he led her down the balcony steps into the garden.

"Miss Rothsby is here?"

"Yes, but Lord Beauvoir escorted us."

Because of her distress, Dash kept himself and his jealousy in check. But he would never allow her to leave with the puffed-up dandy. He wasn't letting her go again if he had any say.

"I can't be seen going into the garden with you alone. Not with your reputation."

"Now you're worried about our reputations." He struggled not to say any more. "I plan to seat you on that bench." He pointed to the stone bench in view of anyone from the balcony. "And then I plan to return to the ball and determine whether Roddy made an appearance with our hostess. All this stress might be for naught. You are not naïve enough not to consider the reason your brother hasn't returned home is because of a woman." He couldn't reassure himself when his spine was tingling, and his nerves were flinching.

"Something is wrong. I can feel it. I might not see Roddy for days. He is always busy, but Reese always reports his comings and goings to me even when he has a mistress."

She sat on the bench and gazed up at him. Just as she did when she was a young girl. Her gorgeous eyes trusting him.

He raised her cold hand and pressed it to his lips. "I will find him, Perdita. I promise you. I'm sure there is a logical reason for his absence."

She lowered her face, trying to hide the tears dripping on her cheeks. "You don't believe it any more than I do."

"I will send Miss Rothsby to sit with you until I can escort you home."

Chapter Ten

FOREBODING HUNG IN Dash's carriage like the heavy fog that wafted in from the Thames, turning the night into a surreal dream. Dita couldn't stop shivering. She swallowed and willed herself to gain control. Her body, like her mind, careened in and out of panic mode. Dash's arm was around her, pressing her tight against his hot body, but it made no difference to the icy chill pervading her body and spirit.

Emmy sat stone silent, her lips pursed in disapproval of the impropriety of Dash's jacket and arm draped around Dita. Dash and Emmy had the foresight to take Dita out the garden gate, saving her from providing a spectacle for tonight's guests.

"Did Lord Beauvoir accept your fabrication? He doesn't seem like a man easily hoodwinked by someone of your reputation." Emmy rarely used her stern vicar's daughter's tone in Dita's company, but she wielded it as well as Dita did her sticks and knives. And it currently was aimed directly at Dash.

"No sane man would question my word, Miss Rothsby." Dash's harsh voice lashed in the small space as did the wind that was picking up. The tension in his stiff posture and clenched jaw filled the airless carriage.

"Because you will meet them on the field of honor if they do, my lord?" Emmy asked sweetly, pushing her glasses up her nose.

Why was Emmy baiting the bear? Dita was too overwhelmed to

join in the skirmish.

"Lord Beauvoir should have been the gentleman to escort Dita home. There will be speculation about your part in this drama." Emmy gazed out the carriage.

"I made sure that everyone heard that my good friend Lord Clifton had entrusted me to escort his sister home after Lady Perdita had received distressing news about her dear cousin. It will be spread through the ballroom."

"You are very skilled in dissembling, my lord."

"Dearest, I care not about the talk. Roddy is in trouble." Dita hated that her voice quivered. Hated that she wasn't in command of herself and needing to lean into Dash's heat and strength. She had been handling everything on her own, and practice over the years had made her very good at it. But tonight, she didn't have the reserve or the will to fight. Maybe it was because she had spent the last days ignoring the rising fear that something was amiss, hoping that her instincts were wrong.

A great weight had been lifted by Dash's exit of Haversham's this morning when she believed that Roddy, too, was at the club. If she hadn't run to avoid public discovery, she would have not wasted the day on frivolities instead of continuing the search. She had to believe that she would know in her heart if Roddy was dead. If she didn't have that hope…

"What if Lord Beldon's conjecture that Roddy has a new mistress is correct, and all this worry is for naught? I must consider all possibilities if I'm to protect you and your reputation."

Dita stared into her dearest friend's eyes, seeing her own worry and fear reflected back at her. Emmy too cared about Roddy and was upset. Emmy reverted to the vicar's daughter, not knowing how else to be of help.

Dita had to pull herself together for both their sakes and for Roddy. But panic had settled into her being and couldn't be shaken readily. Roddy had been her savior in her childhood, as was the man whose muscular thigh was pressed against hers. Both men had been her knights in shining armor, breaking the monotony of a succession of governesses. And tonight, like in the past, Dash's presence helped Dita not to feel alone.

"Emmy, I wish it were true, but my feelings…" She shook her head, struggling for words to express the twisting in her stomach and the bone deep knowledge that Roddy didn't have a mistress. She wasn't a woman given to flights of fancy. She hadn't a childhood spent in girlish daydreams and fanciful play, but rather, hours spent with Alfie in the stable or in the field practicing her skills with the stable boys.

"I'd celebrate any woman that has kept my brother from home. Either he was set upon by footpads when he went to Haversham's or his work for the government has endangered him." A vision of Roddy lying injured in an alley sent a shiver cascading through her.

Dash patted her hand as if he knew her disturbing thoughts. "There is a chance that Roddy might have been called away for a secret government meeting."

Dita appreciated Dash's attempt at comforting her, but he hadn't been able to hide his shock and alarm when he learned of the note. He quickly regained control of himself though repressed restlessness radiated off him. His chin thrust and taut neck conveyed all he didn't express.

"I must search his desk once we arrive at Clifton house for any communication he might have had with Hawkesbury or Sidmouth. Have you spoken to his man of business? He might know of a planned meeting that you weren't privy to." Dash rattling off his thoughts was another sign of his shock.

"Yes, I've spoken with Mr. Potts, his secretary, and he knows nothing that would take Roddy away. And he hasn't spoken to him since Roddy received the note. But if it were government business, Mr. Potts might not be informed." Having to focus on what actions she had taken and still needed to be done kept dread from engulfing her.

"I've already searched his office. There is nothing which gives any hint of what he was working on. Of course, a set of fresh eyes will help, but I believe his office in Westminster may hold a key to this business. His secretary wouldn't allow me access to his office without Roddy present—after he recovered from his shock at my appearance at the male bastion. But I'm sure you'll be able to get past his secretary." Dita relived the embarrassment and powerlessness she felt under Roddy's secretary's scrutiny when she requested to remain in Roddy's office until he returned. She wanted to search the office and hadn't wanted to alert anyone that Roddy might have returned to gambling and womanizing with his dissolute friend.

"You went to Westminster? And wherever else have you gone risking yourself?"

She resented his tone that she was somehow at fault.

"It is not unseemly to visit her brother at his work. I accompanied her." Emmy was like a ferocious watch dog, ready to attack for her mistress.

"Did you find it unseemly for Lady Perdita to be at Haversham's this morning disguised as a servant?"

"My goodness. Was it only this morning?" Dita waded between the opponents. "I also sent messages to White's and Gleason's Boxing Club knowing I would never gain admittance. Roddy didn't respond to either note." Roddy had also been educated in the arts of self-defense by Alfie. Of course, Alfie refused to tutor her seriously in boxing. Only women of lower classes were allowed to strike each other in the face. Not that Dita had any desire to hit anyone but right now… there was always tomorrow.

UPON ARRIVAL AT home, Dash blasted out of the carriage, lent a hand to Dita, and then to Emmy. His need for action resonated with Dita. She too wanted to do something and not just be a shivering mess.

"Lady Perdita?" Reese stood with the door open. The butler, like Totty, had been with the family since she was a little girl. His mouth was agape at Dash's jacket around her shoulders. "Is anything amiss, my lady? Should I summon the physician?"

Dash took her arm and marched her down the hallway. "Summon Totty, Reese. Lady Perdita has had a shock," he spoke over his shoulder. "We'll be in the library."

"Dash, I'm capable of speaking to the servants." She pivoted, pulling out of Dash's grip. "Please do not summon Totty, Reese. It is very late. Rosetta and Emmy will assist me." And she linked her arm with Emmy instead. "I think we are both in need of fortification."

"A thimble size only," Emmy quirked, imitating her father, who publicly disdained drink but enjoyed a snifter or two. "I believe I will pass on spirits tonight. Shall I summon Rosetta to draw you a bath?"

"Not yet. Beldon and I need to search Roddy's library."

Dita wasn't convinced there was anything new for Dash to find. "Good evening, Billy." The earnest youth was standing on alert and had swept the doors open as they approached.

"Billy, can you build the fire? Her ladyship is chilled," Dash commanded.

Dita took off his jacket and handed it to him before seating herself in front of the fire that Billy was igniting into snapping flames. The library provided comfort with all the memories she and Roddy shared here. She had to believe that Roddy would soon be sitting across from her. He had appeared more than tired when she replayed their last night together. Had he known of the danger he would get into? A chill swept through her despite her close position to the roaring fire.

Dash threw his jacket over one of the chairs before striding to the side table with the decanter, glasses, and the bottle of Roddy's best French brandy. His powerful form and his confident manner diminished the shadows hovering in the room.

He poured a large snifter and proceeded to hand one to Dita. "Tonight has been difficult for you. This will heat you and help you sleep."

She didn't want to dull herself with too much drink, but a sip or two would help to warm her.

Dash didn't pour himself a drink but went to Roddy's desk and began to sift through the papers scattered on the desk.

"You waste your time. There is nothing of import. You should leave for Haversham's. There lies the mystery."

"I see that the brandy has restored your color and your need to direct me." Dash's voice held no rancor when he looked up from the papers. "Is Alfie in London?"

"Alfie? He left last week for Sussex but will return next week. There are a few mares he wanted to check on."

Dash, like a stallion fighting the bit, strode across the room in his efficient manner but with barely suppressed energy. "I want to have a few men guarding the house tonight until I can bring my men."

A frisson of fear spiked down Dita's spine as her brain scrambled to grasp why there would be a threat against the household.

"Do you fear the servants or I are in danger?"

"I don't believe there is a great risk, but I'd rather be vigilant until we have this sorted out."

"There will be questions about assigning the men to patrol the grounds." Tomorrow she would have to address the household. Not wanting to frighten them, she needed to make them aware of the danger.

"We don't need to share the news of Roddy yet. I will tell the servants that there have been burglaries in the neighborhood. And it would be best not to confide in anyone but Totty and Reese. I feel we should trust no one. And in the morning, it would be good to check with Totty if anyone or anything has been suspicious. I will check with Reese about unexpected guests on my way out."

Dita didn't like the implication that their servants couldn't be trusted, but Dash was correct in using caution. "I just remembered that Roddy had a late-night visitor. At the time, it was surprising. He often had unusual visitors late at night before he left for France, but few since he returned. Coming home late from a soiree, I stopped at the library door to see if Roddy was still awake. I couldn't hear much but they spoke in French, and Lord Yardley was mentioned several times and the name Carolina. On the night of our ball, I saw Yardley coming out of the library when Roddy was in the ballroom. It struck me as odd at the time, but then I forgot about it with all the demands of the ball. Do you think Lord Yardley is involved with Roddy's disappearance?"

Dita considered sharing their information about Lord Yardley's gambling debts, but Dash probably was aware of all the men like himself who owed Haversham.

Dash's eyes narrowed and a harshness clouded his face. "Did you speak to Roddy about Yardley in the library?"

"No." She didn't want to admit that all she could think about after the ball was Dash.

"I will pursue Yardley." Dash moved to stand in front of her.

"I will send a message to Alfie to return to London, but it may take him a few days." Dita needed her mentor with her at this time. Dita met Dash's eyes, sharing an intimate understanding of the role Alfie played in her life.

Dash bent and, for a minute, captured in his caring gaze, she thought he might kiss her. He lifted her hand to his lips. "I promise you that I will not stop until Roddy is safe at home."

The air in the room thickened. Her heartbeat crashed against her chest violently, echoing in her ears. All her words were gone. All she was capable of was a slight nod, unable to break the connection. He was as trapped as she was in the intense force, unable to release her hand or her stare. His throat worked in a slow undulation.

He sat on the couch and lifted her onto his lap. "I can't leave you like this. You have no reason to trust me. But if our past means anything to you, you must know that I will never leave you alone. You will always have me in whatever way you decide for our future. I will never stop protecting you."

She should protest the way he handled her, but the clean smell of his linen shirt, his heat surrounding her, and the earnestness in his voice steadied her.

"Why?" After all the years, all she could utter was one word.

"You don't have to forgive me, but I want you to know the

reason I severed our relationship. I can't allow you not to know the truth, especially now. After I assumed the title, I learned that my father had gambled away my inheritance. I was left penniless to cover the expenditures of the estate with no money. Hundreds of workers and servants depending on me for their livelihood. The bastard died, leaving me with his mess."

"It must have been an awful shock. But it still doesn't explain why you needed to act alone."

"I didn't want you anywhere near the disgrace when the *ton* discovered the state of my finances. I loved you too much."

"You loved me? It didn't feel like it at the time." She didn't leave her room for a week after he left her, refusing to eat or speak with anyone. It was Alfie who dragged her literally out of her room and out of her misery. He helped her channel her broken spirit into her martial arts.

"I was filled with rage and believed I was destined to become my father." He stared at the fire, avoiding eye contact.

Perdita wanted to tell him that nothing mattered but their love. That they could have faced it together. But Dash hadn't needed her in a crucial moment in his life.

"You can't understand—and I hope you never will—what it was like to grow up with a parent that hates you. You believe that you're at fault no matter how much you try to please them." He took her hand and rubbed his thumb along her palm. Lost in his thoughts, he didn't seem aware of his actions.

"Now that I'm older, I understand that my father hated himself. But when I realized the only means to recoup the losses and save the estate was to gamble using my mathematical skills, it reinforced all my deepest fears. I was destined to be Beldon, a drunk and a gambler."

"But why didn't you tell me? I loved you. We could have married and used my dowry to help your estates." Her voice quivered as the deeply buried pain surfaced. "You made me feel lovable and then left me. My parents might not have actively hated me, but their neglect was the same."

"Oh, darling. I know I hurt you, but you must believe at the time, I thought you were better off without me. I couldn't ask you to sacrifice yourself. The shame I felt being the angry, lonely boy who needed rescuing was nothing I wanted to feel again. I couldn't ask you to save me. Again."

"It was your pride and your inability to trust me…" She didn't want to relive all the pain she saw reflected in his eyes and heard in his voice.

"I did trust you because I knew exactly what you would want to do—marry me and use your dowry. Roddy would have allowed the marriage since he was my friend and would have wanted to help too. And I couldn't let you. Not out of pride. Knowing my family heritage, I never believed I deserved you even when I was destined to be a wealthy earl. But forcing you to marry me to save the estate, knowing someday you might regret or resent the choices I took from you was unbearable. You were so young."

Would she have regretted marrying Dash? She wasn't given a choice. She loved him and would have done anything for him. She hated having to accept any part of Dash's reasoning. She wanted to hate him because if she didn't her whole world was tilted upside down.

"And without me and any scandal associated with your name, you have become an incredible woman, the toast of the Season, able to choose anyone." He smiled at her, the worry lines around his eyes softening as he pressed a kiss to her hand.

A glimpse of the tender, gentle Dash that she had loved was so familiar it hurt. She could believe the younger and loving Dash thought he was doing the right thing. Leaving her, he had forced her to grow in ways she never imagined and had made her stronger. If she had married, she would have children by now and no chance of starting a spy school. She always fantasized about having a large family with Dash, both committed to never letting their children suffer as they had.

"I had planned to win back my fortune and then beg your forgiveness… but then unplanned circumstances intervened. You must believe that not everything about me is true. I can't yet share with you the reason why I must present myself as a degenerate drunk and gambler in society. Once we have Roddy home, I will explain and allow you to decide my fate. Our fate."

Her brain was buzzing like a hive of agitated hornets. Was a future possible with Dash after all the hurt? They had both changed. "It is a lot to absorb."

"It was selfish of me to tell you any of this tonight. Forgive me. All I wanted you to know is that you can depend on me to protect you and find Roddy. You have me. Always will." He pressed another kiss to her hand. "There is nothing more for you to do tonight. You need to rest. I will return tomorrow and tell you everything I've learned at Haversham's."

Lost in her thoughts and the magical force surrounding them, his plans didn't register. He wanted her to go to bed and do nothing. She pulled her hand away to stand, needing to assert herself. "You must come back after Haversham's. I will not sleep without knowing what has transpired. Promise me you'll return." She couldn't retire when she could help.

"It will be tricky work and may require hours. You've suffered a shock and need to rest."

"You have also experienced a shock. Do you need to rest?" She arched her perfectly shaped eyebrow. "I will sleep when Roddy is home."

"Pig headed," he muttered under his breath but loud enough for her to hear. "I will return when I'm finished, but until then, promise me you'll attempt to sleep. And you're not to leave this house."

"Yes, my lord. I am yours to command." She curtsied, keeping her gaze down as a woman of breeding was expected to behave. The submissive position hid her smirk, knowing that Dash didn't believe her obedient act. It was a game they had played as children.

His loud chuckle had her looking up. The blasted man had the nerve to be grinning.

"If only it were true, Perdita." He raised one arched eyebrow in imitation and leaned closer. "It is one of my favorite fantasies." His voice was husky and laced with innuendo.

Dita's breath quickened at his promise and his closeness. Then he ruined it by batting her nose with one finger as if she were a child. "Rest." And he was gone without a backward glance, the sound of his footsteps echoing down the hallway before Billy closed the door.

She was a stew of emotions and wasn't sure she could discuss Dash with Emmy, feeling like she failed her friend by responding so easily to Dash, whom Emmy saw as a heartless rake. Their connection was complicated by past emotions and staggering desire and now his revelations. She had so many questions. And Dash had just complicated it more by pledging his love and denying his reputation. It was too much of everything to sort through. She had to focus on Roddy.

"Well, I'm definitely not going to rest," Perdita spoke aloud to the empty room. "You would be tearing London apart if I disappeared, and I won't fail you, Roddy."

She needed to come up with her own plan of action while Dash pursued the gambling club. But first, she must get out of her ballgown. She couldn't think with stays poking her ribs and hairpins sticking into her skull. She would not get any sleep with Roddy missing and her need to rehash every word and touch shared with Dash.

Chapter Eleven

DASH RAPPED HIS fist on the carriage roof to stop. Haversham's was clogged with gentlemen who had done their duty and now were ready for more male pursuits. The staff would be overwhelmed with the arrival of the pleasure-seeking men, giving him the perfect cover to ask questions.

From his taller stature, he was able to see over the group of young bucks who waited in a queue to gain admission. Haversham stood at the door greeting the future of England, which at this moment didn't stir confidence with their loud, uncouth behavior. He winced at the memory that he had behaved in the same manner at that age, believing himself to be quite daring. Waiters hovered close by to offer drinks to the men who needed no further liquor. They had already enjoyed more than Lady Billingsworth's watered-down fruit punch.

Haversham, a savvy businessman, knew that spirits meant men took more risk and gambled with little attention. Over-imbibing helped men along the path to stupid decisions. Which of the group would ruin his future and curse tonight's folly for years to come?

The atmosphere was one of a university pub. Ribald comments and challenges laced the air. Escaping the forced politeness of the balls, the youths were ready to shed their gentlemanly behavior and seek unrestrained adventures to prove their manhood.

Waiting for the entrance to be cleared, Dash cursed under his breath. His timing was off all night. First arriving too early at the ball and now to appear unaffected by the ridiculous scene in front of him when all he wanted to do was take Haversham to a dark alley and beat the answers out of him. Dita's distress stirred everything savage in him. He had never seen her so undone. The only other time he had seen that look of utter vulnerability was the night he severed their relationship. The way she battled the shock and pain, fighting not to cry, her gorgeous eyes glassy with unspent tears. What he would do to undo that moment. It had been out of his hands. But now he would die before he allowed her to suffer further. Roddy's life depended on Dash remaining his usual methodical and careful self and not ruled by his feelings. But having Dita in the mix was testing all his resolve.

Upon spotting Dash, Haversham directed the boisterous crowd to move aside and allow him entry. Spending enormous amounts of England's money at the club gained him special treatment.

"Haversham, tonight will fill your already well-lined coffers."

Dressed in his signature outfit, a red brocade waistcoat and black coat with an open collar with no cravat, Haversham closely examined Dash's formal wear. At least Dash had pulled apart his valet's sculpted cravat, which now hung loose around his neck. Tonight's blue silk waistcoat and black coat were in deep contrast to Dash's usual unkempt black dress. The fact wasn't lost on Haversham.

"Oh, the rumors are true." Haversham grinned, unfazed by his missing front tooth.

"To which might you be referring? There are so many." Dash adopted his weary attitude. "Gossip is spread by wicked people." Dash paused. "Proverbs 16:28, in case you don't know your Bible."

Dash doubted that Haversham had ever attended church or

opened a Bible. "And what wicked tale am I the center of tonight? The latest about you is that you've reconciled with your half-brother the duke." Old Leicester never acknowledged Haversham since his mother was a prostitute at a local brothel. His son, the present duke, abhorred the scandal and shunned Haversham.

Haversham didn't flinch with the insult. Unless one paid attention, he wouldn't catch the slight narrowing of the club owner's glare and an almost imperceptible shift to the right. But Dash was paying attention.

"As true as you are in need of a rich wife." Haversham was aware of everyone's debts including Dash's.

"Touché." Dash glanced at the hazard table before meeting Haversham's eyes. "I'm to meet Clifton here. Has he arrived yet?"

Haversham returned Dash's stare with nary a blink. The only reaction was his jaw muscles tightening before he diverted his gaze to the crowd. "I haven't seen him tonight." His voice didn't change in inflection. "Yardley, Vinson, and Weber have arrived if you're looking for a game."

Haversham bowed his head in false deference and headed to the crowd of bucks.

Dash, caught in the rowdy crowd moving *en force* to the tables, almost staggered at the weight of someone falling into him. Dash twisted to warn off the drunken fool.

"Sorry, ole man. In a rush and all that." Frankland shrugged, his eyes red with drink.

Dash had to control the urge to not wring the bastard by his cravat.

Frankland, unaware of his peril, leaned closer, reeking of brandy. "You sly dog, bagging the prize of the Season. I saw you making nice as if... offering the lady your jacket."

"One more word out of your mouth, and you'll never see your mother again."

Dash didn't get enough satisfaction from how quickly Frankland paled and stuttered. "I meant… my apologies." He backed up and quickly blended into the crowd.

If it weren't for protecting Perdita's reputation in this morning's fiasco, he'd have Frankland and Cole in the alley right this moment. Perdita did not need her name linked with his at this time. He was helpless to intervene in rumors were it ever discovered that she had been near Haversham's. Anything he might say would only escalate the gossip.

Impatient on this fool's errand of getting anything from Haversham, who was a skilled manipulator and liar, Dash pushed through the gathered men. He had to get into Haversham's office. It was unlikely he would discover anything in the club. After gathering impressions from Yardley and Vinson about Roddy, he would assess the best way to break into Haversham's sanctuary.

The area was well guarded. Men would kill to gain access to the ledgers stored there, containing every titled gentleman's true fortune. And a few years ago, Dash would have done anything to prevent the knowledge of his estate to be revealed.

Dash wasn't as interested in the ledgers as he was in finding the reason Haversham sent the note to Roddy. It didn't add up that Haversham would implicate himself if he was behind the kidnapping.

From his years of play, Dash knew the schedule of everything that happened at the club. He also was friendly with Whitaker, Haversham's man of business, who handled the ledgers. Every night, Whitaker sat at the table at the back of the club, keeping meticulous records of each gentleman's debts. And at closing in the early morning, Whitaker took the ledger to the safe in Haversham's office upstairs. The office also had an exterior stairwell that led to the alley near the club's large stables reserved for the guests.

The best chance of breaking in would be after the man of business had taken the books upstairs and the men were departing. There was always a flurry of activity, making it the best time to search. The guards would be distracted, tired, and not expecting any intruders after the ledgers were secure in the safe. Dash would enter by the alley entrance.

Making his way to his table, Tessa, a prostitute who was newly arrived in the past six months, smiled at Dash. The young woman, barely out of her teens, sauntered through the crowd selling her wares as Haversham required. Dash at first had taken her under his protection, pretending to hire her only to take her upstairs to spare her from the demands of the other men.

After his father died, he'd spent a few months of heavy drink and whoring at Haversham's, trying to suppress all the pain and rage. He never considered how little choice many of the prostitutes had until witnessing a young woman fresh from the country who took her own life within weeks of working the club. From that point on, he made it part of his mission to supplement the young women's income to give them a chance to get away from Haversham who kept a careful watch on his "property."

Tessa was heading toward Dash when Randolph grabbed her from behind and pulled her into his lap. The young woman pushed against the old lecher's chest, trying to escape. The bastard was old enough to be Tessa's grandfather and had a young wife and a mistress. Dash's limits were being pushed. He sauntered to Tessa, who struggled, making Randolph laugh. Dash took her hands and pulled her to stand, extricating her out of Randolph's clutches.

"Randolph, a lady likes to have a choice," Dash warned.

"Lady?" Randolph snorted.

"Maybe you didn't hear me over the noise." Dash never wavered in his deathly stare fixed on the baron.

"No harm done." The old blustering fool smiled with his yellowed teeth and grizzly chin.

"Thank you, my lord." Tessa looked at him through her long golden eyelashes. Her eyes were heavily painted with kohl and her lips with rouge to mark her profession.

He took her arm and led her toward the stairs. "Tell the other gentlemen that you are taken for the evening." Handing her a handful of coins, he lowered his voice. "This is enough to keep Haversham happy for a while."

Relief covered her face. "I'm happy to accommodate you, my lord."

"Tessa, we've been over this. You are to save your money and return to your village."

He always paid her over what Haversham expected, so she would eventually have enough to return to her family. And in turn, she told him what secrets she was made aware of in the club. He hadn't planned to use her as an informant, but she was very observant and would share gossip to be entertaining, not realizing how helpful her information could be.

"Haversham is looking." He crushed her against him. He lowered his head, giving an appearance of a lover. "Have you heard anything mentioned about Lord Clifton or a kidnapping?"

Her eyes widened, and she reached up to smooth his hair. "Can you meet me later in the alley?"

This had to be important since he had never met her outside. They never discussed anything upstairs. Haversham had holes in the walls so his men could watch and report information used later for blackmail. Usually, she was able to share tidbits in passing, climbing the stairs, or sitting on his lap as he gambled.

"When everyone is staggering out in the morning is the best time. No one will notice that I'm gone."

"Go upstairs before one of these randy fools comes after you." He swatted her on the arse, in case Haversham still watched.

Tessa giggled and said loudly, "I will be waiting for you, my lord."

Dash sorted through the possible information Tessa could have and how she obtained it. Could this be what he needed to find Roddy? For a brief moment, he envisioned Perdita's joy at her reunion with Roddy.

"I might have to try that young whore if she can distract a hard-ened cad like yourself, Beldon." Weber patted the sweat rolling down his forehead. The idea of the lecher pawing sweet Tessa sickened him.

"I like him distracted. Gives me an advantage in the game." Yardley smirked.

"It might be imprudent of you, Beldon, if Lady Perdita learns of your lady love before you are married. Or her brother. Clifton is a conservative kind of fellow. Nothing like his father." Vinson drew on his cigar, watching Dash. "You're exactly like your father." Vinson, a small fastidious man with impeccable dress and manners, was the quiet observer but as sleazy as his chums.

Dash dropped to the empty chair.

"Clifton is a good friend of Beldon. I'm sure he'll approve of the match—despite your reputation… I was hoping he would accompany you tonight." Yardley searched Dash's face.

"I'm surprised as you are that he isn't here. I missed him at Lady

Billingsworth's ball. Did you speak with him?" Dash took a sip of the brandy that appeared as soon as he sat. He relaxed against the back of the chair.

"Last time I saw Clifton was at White's. He was with Pitt and his minions. Not sure what Pitt is up to. Seeking Clifton's support to become the next prime minister? An interesting proposal since our former prime minister was against the treaty that Clifton spent a year working on." Vinson shuffled the cards. His long slender fingers were effeminate, as were his manners.

"Clifton has been in Pitt's pockets for a while now. Planning ahead for his own career, I believe," Weber added. "Pitt won't sit on the sidelines too long."

Interesting that Yardley didn't volunteer any information. But Vinson was very helpful in giving Dash a new avenue to search. Maybe Roddy's absence was in fact to do with his diplomatic work and nothing to do with Dash and his involvement at Haversham's. His highly developed instincts told him the opposite. Haversham was somehow involved, but kidnapping a well-respected earl with a century-old title was taking a big risk. And Haversham was many scurrilous things, but he was foremost a businessman. So why take the risk?

Dash searched the cards he was dealt. Not a bad hand. No one appreciated that it was harder for him to lose than to win. He was eager for this part of the night to be finished, so he could speak with Tessa and hopefully have good news for Perdita. He discarded his ace, ruining any chance of winning.

Chapter Twelve

DITA, DRESSED IN riding breeches, a jerkin, and with her curls pinned and tucked into a cap, sat in the back of the small, unmarked carriage bearing no identification. After hours of waiting for Dash to return, she could stay home no longer. She had napped for a brief time but awakened with the awful crushing sensation in her chest when remembering Roddy was missing.

She had paced for another hour by the early morning light before concluding that Dash might not come for hours. She then dressed to take Buttercup to Rotten Row and work out the anxiety that plagued her. She needed action, and Alfie wasn't here to spar with her to burn off her endless energy.

When in the stables, a memory from the night in the library surfaced. Her brother had directed Reese to ready his horse to ride to Haversham's. Harry, the assistant stable master, confirmed that Roddy had ridden his stallion that night. Fury was a beast if not handled properly and would be memorable at any stable. And Fury, like Roddy, hadn't returned.

With the missing horse as a possible clue, she decided to act. She had to go to Haversham's where she would wait for Dash to exit. They could then search Haversham's stable for the stallion. She was dressed like a stable hand to accompany Dash. He wouldn't recognize the horse and wouldn't know if Haversham's men were lying to him. She knew Fury very well and was capable of handling the headstrong horse.

Dash would not be happy with her arrival. She considered send-ing a note of her plans, but what if it was intercepted? This could be a real breakthrough and couldn't be ignored. She wasn't a silly woman running off on a hare-brained scheme as Dash might accuse her of. She was using extreme caution. She brought her knife, which was tucked into her waistband. Her position in society constrained active spying, but there were ways around society as she had proven in her disguise as a servant and now as a stable hand. Harry drove the carriage and was also trained by Alfie in self-defense. The stableman had bulk and strength, which Dita didn't. He would be able to help if needed.

She closed her eyes and willed her thrashing heart to slow. She had spent her awake hours replaying the evening that Roddy disappeared. He had thrown the note into the fire, which was unusual. Was he keeping secrets from her? Had he lied to her about Haversham's and Dash? But if he had government business, why wouldn't he have shared this information with her? She did question him a lot about the war, but he was adept at avoiding anything he didn't want to answer. There was no reason for him to lie to her. She tried to squelch her hurt feelings that Roddy didn't believe she could be trusted. And maybe if Roddy had, she wouldn't be desperately searching for clues to his whereabouts.

She had questioned Reese about the person who had delivered the note. He had told her that Dash had asked him the same. A street urchin who was paid by a "toff" delivered the note to the servants' quarters. There was nothing to pursue with the note, but finding Fury in Haversham's stable would confirm that the note Roddy received was a fake to lure him to the club.

Light streaked through the window. Dawn was quickly approaching. Dash must have finished by now. What if he didn't come out of Haversham's to accompany her to the stables? She'd do what needed to be done. She was well trained.

Dita yawned at the same time her stomach grumbled. She had no appetite but probably should have eaten something besides the tepid tea she had shared with Emmy the night before. Emmy was going to be mad that Dita had left her out of this morning's excursion. She hadn't thought of Fury until she arrived at the stables. And how could Dita, dressed as a stable boy, have her companion accompany her? Emmy didn't have the skills required this morning. No matter the logic, Emmy's feelings would be hurt.

It was too bad Charlotte, with a theatrical bent and a flair for disguises, wasn't in London. She could have accompanied Dita. Not accepted into polite society with her unknown patronage, Charlotte remained in Bath as a teacher at Miss Danvers' school. The boldest of the four girls, she hoped to work undercover in France, and this morning would be a perfect experience for her.

Charlotte had coached the others about living in the disguise like a character on the stage. Dita was not a good actress, but she had no trouble acting the part of a stable boy. She had grown up wearing this outfit to ride horses and to practice her fighting skills with Alfie. She truly had benefited from her parents' neglect in having a freer childhood than other young women of her station. She'd always longed for love from her mother and father, but Alfie, Harry, Reese, and Totty had offered affection when her parents were incapable or unwilling.

Dita's hunger, thirst, and nervousness intensified with the more time she spent alone in the carriage. How much longer would she have to wait? She had been parked across the street from the club for over an hour. Dita found herself drifting off, thinking of Dash's vow that he loved her. The sensitive and attentive man from last night was the man she had loved. Their incendiary kisses at the ball had reawakened the physical needs that she had denied herself. The pleasure in his arms at the ball, mixed with the memories and his promises, reawakened a flittering feeling of hope. But could she trust him with her feelings? She wasn't sure she could live through the pain of his betrayal again.

He was wounded by his childhood and by his loss of fortune, but he had spent the past years in a gambling den and had one of the worst reputations in all of society as a wastrel and a rake.

Emmy reported that the rumor blatant in Lady Billingsworth's ballroom was that Dash had returned to the *ton* to marry Dita for her dowry. Did he believe he could kiss her and beg her forgiveness, and the past would be forgotten and the present ignored? Had he changed so much that he could manipulate her, pretend kindness, and make promises of love to regain her trust? Her inability to not respond to him and his touches and their shared childhood blurred her perspective. She was out of her depth with the seasoned rake.

Dita was startled out of her reverie by the sound of voices. Men were starting to leave the club but no sight of Dash. Carriages were pulling up in front of the entrance, most likely from the stable on the side of the club. This would be the best time to go into the stable, when the staff was busy getting mounts and carriages ready— a perfect time to blend into the confusion.

If she waited too long, her entry would be noticeable. She watched the gentlemen staggering out in the early light. She spotted Frankland and Cole leaving together. She needed to find a way to reveal their true nature to society. Their attack on her would not be forgotten. She would discuss this with Emmy, who was proving quite adept at manipulating society's expectations. The Frenchman's taunt to Dash was brilliant by keeping him off-kilter about her marriage plans and making him jealous.

She leaned out the window opposite the entrance, not wanting to draw attention with her high-pitched voice. She spoke quietly to Harry. "Pull around to the front of the alley. Let's get a view of the activity from the street."

Harry moved the carriage forward and stopped at the entrance to the alley, giving her a view. There was a flurry of men running back and forth, bringing horses out of the enormous stable which was almost the size of the club. It would take time to search for Fury in the extensive area, but at least fewer horses would need to be examined.

Her focus was captured by a couple barely visible in the shadows of the club. All the air went out of her lungs. Not able to catch her breath, like all the times Buttercup, with the disposition of a prickly rose not a delicate buttercup, had thrown her. It was Dash. She would recognize his broad shoulders and the tilt of his head anywhere. He was standing close to a woman, with his hand braced over her head. The position of his arm prevented Dita from seeing the woman's face. His large frame hovered over her, his body and head bent as to a lover. The woman's dress was cut low, and her hair was loose around her shoulders. The sound of the woman's giggle hurt like knives piercing Dita's skin.

Dash curved his head toward the woman to kiss her. Dita was frozen in place, unable to move away from the pain and the need to continue to watch. Memories of Dash's muscular body over hers in the same sensual way and the pleasure of his soft touch on her cheek slammed through her in painful surges. Her heart splintered into tiny pieces.

She wanted to sob, scream, and tackle the traitorous scum to the ground and pummel his lying handsome face and lips.

The cad had told her it was delicate work, and it would take hours. She swallowed hard against the sob twisting up her throat. She had believed him. Again. She had waited for him while he dallied with a prostitute in an alley.

"Harry." She hated that her voice broke. "Drive around to the other side of the stable. There has to be another entrance."

"We should wait for Lord Beldon."

Harry was seeing the same scene as she was. Her friend and compatriot on all sorts of adventures since they were children wanted her to sit in the carriage and witness Dash making love to another woman. Were all men this dense? She had her pride, and she wouldn't allow Harry to know the agony she suffered.

"Drive around to the back. I'm very capable of looking for Fury without any help."

"He might have a very good explanation."

She could hear the disbelief in Harry's tone. He was a loyal friend but not a good liar.

"I might be innocent, but even I recognize lust." Dita couldn't stop herself from looking again. Dash was pushing hair behind the woman's ear—the same way he had stroked her. Her stomach roiled, watching his touch. The one she dreamt of. It had all been an act. All these years, she had believed she was special. Women were interchangeable to the practiced cad. The shame and embarrassment fueled her anger and outrage.

"I'm going to kill the bastard. I'll hang, but I don't care."

"Drive, Harry. He isn't worth your sacrifice, but I appreciate the sentiment." She had the exact same compulsion of killing the lying bastard. She steeled herself not to look as they drove off. Harry took the turn onto the side street next to the stable. They drove to the end of the next alley and stopped next to the stable walls.

Dita opened the door. "I will walk from here."

"Why don't I drive past once to evaluate the activity in the rear?"

"It will take too much time, and someone might see me exiting the carriage. I need to get in there while they are busy." She wanted to get out of the carriage and run as fast as she could away from this place. To outrun the anguish burning in her heart. She was glad to have something to focus on… the misery would come later.

"I should come with you."

"We've already been through this. You will stand out too much. You're a giant and everyone will notice you."

"But Lord Beldon is as big as I am."

Dita didn't want to think of Dash or hear his name. "Yes, but if he is stopped, he is an earl and no one can question his activities." Dash could do anything he wanted, anytime, with anyone he wanted, at any moment. And she had been one of the many.

"Wait for me here and be ready for a possible fast departure."

"When Lord Clifton hears of this, he is going to dismiss me."

The mention of Roddy snapped her out of her self-absorption. Roddy was missing. Her heartache wasn't important. Finding her brother was.

"He won't do any such thing. And you know it. You're delaying me on purpose."

Harry's familiar deep chuckle helped to soothe her raw feelings.

Dita strode away. She would search for Fury, and if the horse was here, she would go to Lord Rathbourne and tell him everything. She didn't need Dash. Aunt Euphemia would ensure she got an audience with Lord Rathbourne.

Dita walked through the back door with a male swagger she'd

acquired from spending time with the stable lads. The main corridor was lined with rows of stalls for the horses. She could see down the path to the front entrance where the carriages were lined up in the alley. This was her chance. No one was at this end. All she had to do was walk down the main corridor and examine the horses in their stalls. She moved quickly, looking back and forth between the sides, hoping for a glimpse of Fury. Many stalls were empty. No sign of the magnificent stallion yet. Would they keep the horse in a hidden space? He was too valuable not to keep. It was possible they had already moved him out of London.

She looked for possible places they could conceal the feisty horse. There were rooms on one side of the building closest to the club. The doors were half open, and she could see the tack and feed rooms. Housing and feeding the large number of horses would require space for the equipage and supplies.

She was halfway down the row when a loud voice from behind her bellowed. "Boy, what are you doing?"

Dita's heart jumped, and she could feel the speeding pulsations in her neck. Panic blasted through her. All her plans stalled somewhere between her brain and her mouth. Was it better to pretend she worked here than announce she was looking for Fury?

She turned slowly, working hard not to touch her cap and to remember to lower the pitch of her voice. "I'm looking for my master's horse. He sent me to get it."

The man strode toward her, his forearms the size of small oak trees bunched under his rolled sleeves. He was a big, muscular man with a misshapen nose and a large scar above his bushy eyebrow. He had the size and strength to easily control any horse, including Fury.

Dita fought the urge to turn and run. But she did back up, edging closer to the front still filled with activity.

"And who be your master?"

She debated what was the best answer. If she had been with Dash, she would have definitely said her brother. Best not to think of the rake at this moment. But without Dash's protection…

Dita inched back and fought the urge to look at the distance to the door. "Lord Clifton is my master. And he wants his horse. Now. He's not a patient man. I don't see Fury. Where is the stallion?"

Something dark and fierce passed across the craggy face. "He sent you, did he? Your master in the club?"

"What does that matter? I need the horse." Did the man hear the way her voice got higher?

He was close enough that the stench of horse manure and sweat filled her nostrils. But it was the antagonism radiating off him that sent big red alerts to her brain. Her muscles tightened, her heart sped, and the taste of fear burned on her tongue.

He inspected her slowly, starting at her dusty worn boots to the cap resting on her forehead.

"You ain't no stable hand. Look at those lily-white hands." He had a long reach, and he lunged forward to grab her.

Darn. She should have spread dirt on her hands. Something to note for the spy classes.

Dita dodged him and took off into a sprint. She could outrun him. She thanked her father for her long legs as her stride outdistanced her bulky pursuer. A smaller version of the grisly giant with well-developed forearms and a misshapen nose came out of a stall and stepped in front of her. "Goin' somewhere?"

"Gentlemen." She stopped and raised her hands as she searched the area for something to defend herself. She had her knife, but it required close combat. Two against one were not good odds, especially when they looked like seasoned brawlers. "Lord Clifton will be very upset that you won't release his horse. No reason to cause yourself problems. He is a very important man. Let me have Fury and I will be gone."

She inched closer to the pitchfork stuck in a hay bale. It was heavier than what she was used to, but it could work if she gripped it high. Screaming for Harry at this point would alert the other men who were busy in the alley saddling horses and hooking horses to their gigs. No one was paying attention to her, and that was what she wanted if she were to escape unscathed.

The bigger guy lumbered slowly toward her. Confident that he would be the winner, he wasn't in any rush. His slow pace gave her enough time to grab the pitchfork and swivel her upper body to swing it over her shoulder to test the weight.

He laughed, his big belly hanging over his rope belt. "This should be entertaining."

She didn't respond but focused all her energy on defending herself. She balanced the instrument in her hand, judging by its weight and greater girth that she would have to use heavier force and a bigger arc than she did with her Kali sticks.

He plodded toward her, raising his ham-sized fists to his chest to pummel her. When he got within hitting distance, she slashed the fork, bringing it high above her shoulder. She swung with all her strength to strike him across the neck, the most vulnerable part of the body. Taking advantage of his surprise, she thrust forward across his middle. He staggered, and she used her offensive position to lunge forward and thrust the pitchfork at his chest. But she hesitated… she hesitated to stab him.

You hesitate, you die. Alfie's words flashed through her mind. She couldn't kill anyone. She couldn't kill the brute just to make her escape.

The smaller guy, who still outweighed her by ten stones, sprung to tackle her. She pivoted and kicked him in the chest. She had strong legs, and the power of her kick had stunned him. He fell sideways, trying to right himself. She rushed forward and, twisting her body to use the momentum, slashed the stick against his temple, another susceptible spot. The thud reverberated in her hands from the force with which she hit him. He fell to the ground, knocked out cold.

If she ran, the giant would yell for others to stop her. Her arms would soon ache from the weight of the stick if she didn't make a quick escape. All she had done to the big brute was incense him. Primal fear pulsed through her veins. Sweat trickled down her back.

The behemoth roared. "You slimy bastard. Fight like a man. Not some namby-pamby using a pitchfork."

Dita accepted that she couldn't stab him. If he got the best of her and was going to beat her, she could pull off her cap and declare who she was. What would the big bully do then? Take her to Haversham? In the least, she'd be ruined, and at the most, she'd be taken prisoner and possibly worse. She had to knock him out quickly and get back to the carriage. It sounded easy in her head. But the reality of her burning muscles and the hatred pointed at her gave her pause. She was becoming too tired to use the stick. She'd have to strike him in the kneecap first, but it meant getting pretty close. He roared again. "I'm going to kick your blimey arse for knocking out Bert."

Anger was a great weapon to turn on your opponent. She took a slow breath, calming herself. Out-of-control emotions were a detriment in a fight. Calm and focused were how Alfie trained her to be.

With his face mottled, he ran straight at her, giving her the perfect opportunity to rotate to her left side and strike him hard straight to the kneecap.

He gasped and keeled over shouting, "Fucking hell. I'm going to tear you apart."

She moved in to deliver the *piece de resistance* and bring her knee up to hit him hard and fast in his manly parts as he bent over.

"Perdita. My God." Dash's voice.

For the one second that she lost her focus, the furious man, oblivious of the knee injury, delivered a punch to her stomach, causing stars to dance before her eyes and the light to flicker on and off in the stable. She tried to keep upright, but the pain blocked out any defense she could muster. She staggered backward, trying to breathe in fractured breaths before the light faded. She felt herself falling into oblivion when suddenly a sharp pain exploded in her head.

Chapter Thirteen

RUSHING TOWARD HER, Dash couldn't grasp what he had just witnessed. Perdita dressed as a man in the stables, fighting off two brawlers. His brain scrambled and still couldn't catch up, watching her take a blow. He ran at full speed toward her. If he hadn't interrupted her, she might not be lying in a heap on the ground. His frozen heart clenched in his chest with the sight of her defenseless and vulnerable. She had lost her cap when she hit her head against the wooden post. Her curls hung partially across her face and around her shoulders. He needed to tend to Perdita, but first, he had to finish the man who had hurt her.

"Blimey hell, that stable lad is a woman." The brute rubbed his knee from the impressive kick she had delivered. "I wouldn't have hit her so hard if I knew she was a stupid twat."

"I'm going to kill you for touching her." Dash walloped the fool in the gut, who put up no resistance since he was still in shock at the revelation that he had been fighting with a woman. The blow staggered the man. Dash was about to finish him off with a facer when he heard a shout.

"No, I'm going to." Harry, Clifton's stableman and Perdita's childhood friend, ran down the aisle. The easy-going man's face was mottled in fury. "Then I'm going to kill you, Beldon... after we get Miss Dita home."

Kneeling next to Perdita, Dash was barely aware of the crunch of Harry's fist to the man's face and the thud of the man hitting the ground. Harry was as big as the bruiser Perdita had taken on. What was she thinking, putting herself at such risk? He would never understand how her brain worked. She wouldn't weigh the risk to herself if anyone she loved was in danger. And tonight was about her brother.

Dash has been about to leave after examining Haversham's records when he spotted Tessa waiting for him. He'd been discouraged—he'd found the name, Carolina, jotted on a sheet of paper but nothing else to help find Roddy.

If Tessa hadn't confirmed that Roddy did arrive at the club, and Dash decided to check for Roddy's horse before returning to Perdita, what would have happened to her? A jolt of pure terror wracked his body when he considered the dire possibilities.

Her eyes were shuttered closed, her lips as colorless as her face. His fervent words were like a prayer spoken in a hushed voice in a confessional. "I'm sorry, darling. I didn't mean to distract you."

His hands trembled as he pushed the curls that had fallen over her eyes. She was so cold. So icy cold and so still. Perdita was never still. She was always in motion, spinning and twirling like a whirligig. He undid the top buttons of her shirt, searching for her pulse. Desperate to feel her life and hoping to have her jump up and laugh as if this was a great prank. He said a silent prayer of thanks at the feel of her slow but steady heartbeat.

He gently lifted her head to feel the back of her skull where she had struck the hard surface. Alarm engulfed him by the wet sticky sensation of her warm blood covering his hand. He reminded himself that head wounds bled profusely. It was her deathly stillness that made it hard to draw air into his lungs. Primitive, heart-slamming fear spread through his veins. He was afraid for the first time in his life. He had faced his own death with less trepidation. He couldn't stop his hands from shaking or the terror clambering in every heartbeat. What would he do in a world without Perdita?

Dash jumped up and tore off the cravat hanging around his neck and then pulled off his coat. He covered her with his coat and then pressed the linen against the open wound. He then carefully lifted her with one arm under her knees. He used his long forearm under her spine, supporting her like a newborn babe. She was tall but he was a big man. She had always fit perfectly in his arms. He applied pressure to the wound, trying to not jostle her with the motion.

"Tell me you have a carriage. You didn't ride here." Dash didn't want to contemplate parading Perdita to the front of Haversham's where his carriage waited. He needed to get her away before the stablemen were done with their chores and returned to the barn and saw their coworkers knocked out.

Harry, who had the smaller fellow by the collar, pointed to the back entrance with one hand. "Yes. It's parked around the side. I'll be there right away after I finish this scum."

The man's voice trembled. "She hit me with a pitchfork. What was I supposed to do? Mr. Haversham don't allow anyone back here."

Dash heard the thump of another body hitting the ground as he took long strides to the exit.

Perdita hadn't stirred with all the motion. Fear was riding him hard. Panic edging on the periphery. Did she have more than a concussion? A bleed into the brain? All because of some crazy notion to do her own investigating.

"I'll be sent to the hulks or transported, but I don't give a damn. I'm going to kill you for hurting her again, you slimy bastard."

Harry had caught up and was shouting at Dash like an unhinged man.

Overpowering Harry wouldn't be easy, but it would relieve the helplessness wedged into his chest. "I'm going to rip you apart limb by limb for bringing her here. Those men in Haversham's employ are ex-boxers."

"You? A weak drunk? You can try. But I'll be the one tearing you apart."

Harry's threats washed right over him. The stableman didn't frighten him in the least. "I shouldn't have shouted at her... but damn it. My God, she was defending herself against that giant." Fear slashed through him without any outlet. "I hold you responsible. You could have stopped her."

"Little do you know her. She would have found a way if I didn't bring her."

Dash felt as if his brain was going to explode out of the top of his head. If his hands weren't filled with a non-responsive Perdita, he'd have his hands around Harry's neck, choking the life out of him. "You fucking blunderhead. You let her walk into the stables alone. What did you think the outcome would be?" Shouting did nothing to help the situation. But yelling at Harry felt good even if he was as distraught as Dash was.

Harry's rage was plastered across his face, his face and neck beet red, his jaw clenched. He rushed ahead to open the carriage door. "I brought her here to see if Fury, Lord Clifton's horse, was in the stables. She waited for you in front of the club to accompany her until she saw you with your doxy. Then there was no stopping her." Harry shook his head in disgust. "You don't deserve to touch her... but I know my place. Once Miss Dita wakes up, you'll never get near her. I'll make sure of it... that is until the earl returns." Harry slammed the door before climbing onto the box.

Perdita moaned either from Dash repositioning her on his lap or from the bellowing and the door slamming. The sound was like the "Hallelujah" chorus in Handel's masterpiece. She was strong and healthy and would recover. No other outcome would be acceptable. He would make sure.

But once awake, how would he explain what she had witnessed? Of course, she saw what he wanted the Haversham's spies to see, a gentleman seducing a prostitute. He couldn't defend himself without revealing his role. She had little faith in him, and tonight proved that she had been right all along.

He cradled her in his arms, trying to warm her with his heat. He bent and kissed her on the top of her head, and the scent of vanilla wafted in his nostrils. "Do you hear me, Perdita? I love you. Only you. I've always loved you."

Perdita groaned with his words.

"You're going to have one hell of a headache when you wake up. But you're going to be fine."

The emptiness of the carriage and the emptiness of the last years without Perdita echoed in his soul. He had been drifting for so long since the day he walked away. He hadn't held or comforted anyone since he left Perdita. He missed holding her and offering the part of himself that had been barricaded for years.

"I never meant to hurt you. None of it was your fault. Nothing but my stupidity." He raised her hand and pressed a kiss to her palm. Her hands were warming. It was a good sign. "We're almost there. Hang in there, darling."

Touching her and calling her darling as he did in the past soothed him more than it did her. He had missed loving and caring for someone. The past three years he'd been so angry, lashing out at life, and throwing himself into his mission to reclaim his family name and help his country. He'd had no time for tender moments. He swore he wouldn't make that mistake again.

Perdita opened her eyes. Dazed, she searched his face before she pressed her hand against his cheek. "Dash?"

"Thank God." Elated, he rubbed his lips against hers. "I'm never letting you go. Ever again."

"This is a wonderful dream. Your lips are as soft as I remember." Her lips turned up as her eyes drifted closed.

His heart swelled with relief, and he relaxed for the first time since seeing her standoff with the stableman. He held her close to him, reveling in the feel of her body against his. There were many nights ahead of them… once he found her brother, and she forgave him for being a self-absorbed fool. But he had overcome bigger challenges.

The carriage hit a pothole, jolting both of them. His hand was dislodged from the back of her head. He had continued to keep the cravat pressed over her wound.

Perdita bolted upright, her eyes wide open. She slowly looked around the carriage and then at him. She examined his face as if she didn't recognize him. And then he knew exactly when the memory of the night, every detail of the past hours including Tessa, came to her. Perdita's open gaze shuttered, and a glower overcame her face.

"You've taken a nasty hit to the back of your head. It is still bleeding." He reached for the cravat that had fallen on the seat to reapply pressure.

She grabbed the cloth from his hand. "Thank you for your assistance. I can do this on my own."

"You need to remain still. You were unconscious for a while and may have brain swelling."

"I don't need to be on your lap to be still." She pushed against his chest to right herself. She gasped with the movement as her hand shot to her side.

"Please, Perdita. There is no reason to cause yourself such pain. The brute hit you hard. He might have broken a rib."

"He didn't. I know what a broken rib feels like, and the pain isn't bad enough."

"You may injure yourself further. Please wait until Dr. Needham can examine you and bind your ribs and tend to your head wound. This is no time to prove your independence." He knew immediately before finishing that he had said the absolute wrong thing.

Her chin lifted and her spine straightened. "Thank you for your concern. I've had plenty of injuries, and neither my head nor my ribs are life-threatening. I am fine to sit on my own for the next few minutes."

Her movements were slow and obviously very painful as she swiveled to place her feet on the floor to leave his lap. He placed his hands on her waist and lifted her onto the seat next to him. He didn't want her to harm herself more.

"Thank you. But once we arrive home, there is no need for your further assistance." She looked straight ahead.

Challenging her independence was the most foolish thing he had done. But the woman scrambled his wits. Why couldn't she be like any other woman who would be grateful to be taken care of? She had swooned when she received the news about her brother but acted as if getting sucker-punched was part of a lady's daily experience.

Perdita, who had spent her childhood running wild with Harry and learning to defend herself from Alfie, was not like any other lady. And it was part of the reason he admired her. She was a warm, loving woman who had all the feminine traits, but she also was a hellion on horseback and, as demonstrated tonight, skilled in defending herself. She went beyond any expectations of what a woman was capable of. And like a stupid, self-destructive arse, he walked away from her.

"Did you see if Roddy's horse was in the stables?" She stared out the window, but her slumped shoulders and her head against the window exposed her attempt to hide her misery.

"I didn't have time, and I doubt Harry did either. But I did learn that Roddy did come to Haversham's asking for me. And Yardley directed him to Haversham's office."

"Oh, this is good news." Her voice lifted. "We'll need to go to the authorities with this information."

"There is no 'we' in this. I will follow up and report everything to you." After tonight, he would not tolerate risking her life.

She twisted to stare at him. She bit her lower lip to hide the pain she must feel from the sudden shift. "Like you did tonight?"

"Harry told me that you saw me with Tessa. It isn't what you think."

"It is of no consequence."

"Perdita, I will explain everything when you are not in pain, and the doctor has examined you. This is not the time for this conversation."

"There will never be a time or need for that conversation. I will never believe anything you say. You have proven your masterful skill at duplicity." The carriage stopped. Harry jumped down and opened the door, looking into the cab.

"Thank God, Miss Dita, that you're awake. You scared me. You were out for so long this time."

Dash had to replay Harry's words. Perdita had been knocked

unconscious before.

"If someone hadn't called my name, the morning would have had a different ending." She didn't deign to look at Dash. Her interest was all for Harry.

"Do you want me to carry you in?" Harry leaned forward, his massive shoulders filling the door.

"It will be the last thing you do." Her lips were pale and pressed together, but she kept up the comradery with her friend.

Harry chuckled. "You're going to need one of Totty's remedies for your headache." He offered his hand to her. She leaned against the wall of the carriage for support as she stood. The strain in her neck and her bent, guarded posture reflected her misery as she took the two steps to the street.

"Harry, no need to share too much with Alfie when he returns. He'll have us both mucking out the stables for months." Perdita put her hand on Harry's arm, which demonstrated her difficulty.

"I can't lie to him. And I'll be the one mucking, not you, if he doesn't send me back to Sussex."

Dash jumped out of the carriage and followed.

Reese opened the door before Perdita and Harry had made it up the next stairs. Perdita was in agony by the way she favored her right side and listed when she walked. The darn woman didn't have to suffer when he could carry her. At least the head wound had stopped bleeding.

"Lady Perdita, what has happened? Did Buttercup throw you?"

"Send for Dr. Needham, Reese." Dash stepped in the entrance, done with acting like a bystander.

"Thank you for your assistance, Beldon. You are not needed any longer. Reese and Totty can take care of me."

"You were unconscious. You will be examined by Dr. Needham.

Reese and Totty will surely see the wisdom. Harry can try to stop me, but he knows you need medical evaluation."

"Fine. Reese, you may send for Dr. Needham. Satisfied?"

"Not in the least." He lifted her into his arms. "You are in pain, and I'm not going to watch you limp up the damn stairs."

Perdita remained stiff in his arms but didn't fight him or speak to him. The silence was deafening. Getting out of the carriage and walking the distance to the house had depleted her last reserves. And he was glad that he had intervened. Not that she would acknowledge any of it. She didn't need to prove her grit to him. He never underestimated her strong constitution.

A footman scurried after them and opened the door to Perdita's bedroom. Miss Rothsby came rushing down the hallway.

"Dita, why is Lord Beldon carrying you? Did Buttercup throw you again?"

Dash was definitely getting rid of Buttercup. Not that this was the battle to be fought at the moment.

"I'll explain everything once we're alone. Can you ring for Totty and Rosetta?"

"Of course."

Dash slowly lowered her to the bed. Miss Rothsby rushed over to plump pillows behind Perdita's back and head. Perdita relaxed on the pillows and closed her eyes.

"I will wait in the library to speak with Dr. Needham after he examines you. And once you've rested, I will be back to have our conversation."

"She's fallen asleep," Miss Rothsby said.

Dash stood and stared at Perdita, who had exhausted herself. "She had a very difficult morning." What an understatement. "Please notify me once Dr. Needham has examined her. I will be in the library."

Having a large stiff drink to calm his nerves. A condition he didn't possess until Perdita came churning hurricane-style back into his life.

Chapter Fourteen

DASH PACED IN the anteroom off the back entrance to Lord Rathbourne's house. It was standard procedure that the intelligence head's "guests" arrived through the alley and were sequestered in small rooms away from the staff and the activity of the household.

Dash was in no mood for sitting. He wanted to get back to Perdita and settle matters between them. He had delayed too long, and he didn't want to wait another moment. It didn't matter that Dr. Needham had given her a dose of laudanum to ease her pain, and she was sleeping. He just couldn't shake the sensation that he needed to be close to her.

He pulled at his cravat. His distressed valet, under pressure to get Dash quickly out of his bloody formal wear, made the knot too tight.

"His lordship is able to see you now, my lord." Brompton, the tall and thin stoic butler whom Rathbourne had acquired in an unusual arrangement as part of his recent marriage, was adept at handling the odd visitors at all hours.

Familiar with the library, Dash strode to the chairs in front of Rathbourne's enormous desk strewn with papers and books.

"I assumed you'd come last night to report this business about Clifton."

It had taken Dash a while to get used to Rathbourne's blunt

style. Sir Ramsey, Rathbourne's predecessor, was a gentleman who liked to sip brandy and discuss the vagaries of the weather before proceeding to the business at hand. Six months after Dash had assumed his title, Ramsey had contacted Dash to offer to secure his father's gambling debts in exchange for maintaining his nightly gambling at Haversham's. Ramsey wanted Dash to observe the club's criminal activities of bribing peers for classified information for the French. Dash had already been a regular and had been slowly winning back his fortune. He had to pace his wins versus his losses not to raise Haversham's suspicion.

Ramsey's proposition to become an undercover agent for His Majesty was an offer of redemption during dire blackness in Dash's life. To be able to save the estate was an offer he couldn't turn down. Many relied on him. He didn't realize at the time, but it also offered him a chance not to traverse the destructive path of his father. Before he worked for Ramsey, Dash had become convinced that Haversham had cheated his father, so bringing the criminal to justice was invigorating. Dash was relieved he hadn't found any evidence that his father had been a traitor. Only that the bastard had been cheated out of the entire estate, and Yardley was most likely part of the scam.

Dash sat, knowing Rathbourne didn't stand on ceremony. The new head was the opposite of his predecessor. Rathbourne was frank and forceful when he had to be. And Dash felt much more comfortable with Rathbourne's style. The rumors were that Rathbourne had been in France after the revolution and was a crack agent. Rathbourne didn't suffer fools easily.

"Petersen sent a man to report an incident that upset Haversham. A lady disguised as a stable boy was searching for Clifton's horse."

Petersen was a card dealer at the club and was one of the men who assisted Dash. The young man reported to Dash anything he observed or heard during the play.

"Oh, hell."

"Haversham was livid when hearing the news and was shouting that he wanted to know the lady's identity."

Foreboding raised the hairs on Dash's neck. "We can't allow Haversham to figure out it was Lady Perdita."

Rathbourne raised one eyebrow. The man used his eyebrows more effectively than a torturer in the Inquisition.

"Damn it. You probably already know that I have a history with Clifton's sister. I'm sure Ramsey shared the whole sordid story. I would have come earlier, but the incident in the stables delayed me. I plan to marry Lady Perdita once we sort out this mess with Roddy." Dash didn't have time to play mental games with his superior. His feelings were too raw. His best friend was missing, his sister sedated from her injuries, and now she'd gained the attention of one of the most dangerous men in London.

"I need to share my assignment with Perdita if I'm to ask her to marry me." He didn't need to explain to Rathbourne that Perdita didn't trust him or consider him a good prospect with his reputation. A reputation that he had ruined for his country. The man was no dimwit. "I will not begin my marriage on a lie. Perdita is a very strong woman and can handle the need for secrecy."

"I'm not surprised she took matters into her own hands with her brother missing. She is an extraordinary lady. She approached me recently with an unusual proposition. Before meeting my wife, I would not have considered the idea."

"She what?" Dash stumbled on his words. He wasn't any more willing than Rathbourne to expose himself or his feelings.

"I don't think it is my role to share her proposition. It was spoken in the strictest confidence." The earl leaned forward, his head resting in his hands with his elbows propped on his desk. "She is very resourceful. And as you know, Lady Perdita's talents are in self-defense."

"She told you of her skill in the martial arts? Why would she share something that is not considered respectable for a lady of her station?" Dash could no longer sit. He shoved out of the chair and paced in front of the desk. "She wants to work for you? She wants to be a lady spy fighting the French with her martial arts?"

Dash paced before the desk, his brain spinning with Perdita's exploits—her disguise as a servant and then a stable boy and using her skills to defend herself. Of course, she would consider herself capable of handling undercover work. He stopped in front of Rathbourne's desk. "Damn it. Tell me everything. She is in danger, and I can't protect her unless I know what she has gotten herself into."

"Up until tonight, Lady Perdita has not done anything to draw attention to herself."

"What has she been doing?" Dash was at the end of his not-so-great patience with Rathbourne acting like a damn smug secretive bastard.

"With the help of her staff and her companion, she has discovered that Lord Yardley is involved in something nefarious. She believes he is involved with the French and communicates with them on the docks."

"How did she find this out?" Images of Perdita down on the docks felt like a kick to the chest, making him freeze in the middle of the room. "She went to the docks?" The docks were teeming with criminals who would show her no mercy.

"No. The ladies use their social activities to gain information. Did you know her companion, a vicar's daughter, can read lips? Miss Rothsby acquired the skill by working with her father's deaf parishioners. She spends her time gathering information at the entertainments Lady Perdita attends. They believe Lord Vinson also plays a part, but they haven't been able to get anything useful."

"My God." Dash's head was about to explode. The woman was going to be the death of him. It was like their childhood with Perdita running amok and no idea of the ramifications. "Lady Perdita is endangering herself and her staff with this nonsense. Does she have any idea how dangerous these men are?" Of course, she did. She had just battled with two ex-boxers and might have won if he hadn't interfered. And earlier she had defended herself from Frankland and Cole.

"I don't consider their information nonsense. She shared their findings to demonstrate the women's abilities to help in our work."

"You can't be considering this ridiculous suggestion. Perdita is a lady and an earl's daughter. This work is below her station as well as dangerous." Spinning with too many emotions, his fear for Perdita clashed with his admiration and respect. She had taken the initiative to be useful in the war with France. She had blossomed into an incredible woman. Not to be one of the ladies who complained how the inconvenience of the war prevented them from acquiring the silks they needed for their ball gowns. How could he not be proud of her? She was smart, strong, and resourceful, and a loose cannon about to detonate. And he never loved her more as he wanted to lock her in his house never to leave again.

"I am considering the idea. Right now, in England, there are ladies of rank who are serving our country with their extraordinary talents." The way Rathbourne's voice warmed made Dash glance up to catch the small smile that crossed his usually severe face. Rathbourne, realizing that he was being observed, returned to his brisk recital.

"Women played a significant role during the French revolution and its aftermath. I have firsthand experience working with female agents. It would be very short-sighted on my part not to use every resource available. And you'd be short-sighted not to consider Lady Perdita's wishes. Her skills and commitment to helping are genuine."

"Over my dead body. I won't tolerate her involvement."

Rathbourne laughed aloud. Dash had never heard the earl laugh. He was always intense and serious. Running an intelligence unit based on deception and lies didn't lend itself humorous moments. "You must decide how you will go forward. But I can say with certainty that you will not be successful by insisting your lady succumb to your demands. The lady will not be swayed. She wants to have a higher purpose than being an earl's daughter. Ignore her wishes at your own peril." Rathbourne chuckled again. Nice to see the man had a sense of humor. If only it weren't at Dash's expense.

Rathbourne raised his hands in defeat at Dash's barely suppressed growl. "I have warned you, but you will have to make your own mistakes."

Dash wanted his superior to promise he wouldn't involve Perdita. He couldn't demand anything from the head or demand anything from Perdita without being her husband. He really couldn't command anything. But her brother could.

"Right now, I have to find Clifton." Dash had to prioritize his challenges, and Roddy took precedence. But he and Perdita would have their reckoning. "Does Clifton's disappearance have to do with his diplomatic work with Hawkesbury? Is there a chance that he couldn't share his mission with his sister?" Dash already knew that more was in play. But he still clung to the futile hope that it was all a misunderstanding and Roddy would appear.

"I'm not aware of any clandestine operations involving Clifton. Ramsey was in charge of the security for the delegation in France. Hawkesbury and Clifton were there only as diplomats. We would never risk interfering in the peace-making process."

Dash wasn't privy to all aspects of the undercover work in France, but he did not doubt Ramsey had many people gathering intelligence during the deliberations and were interfering as much as they could. Rathbourne was supervising the agents to find any and all information about Napoleon, his top advisors Talleyrand and Fouche, and their plans for invading England.

"Then the only conclusion for Roddy's disappearance is his association with me and my work at the club." Dash refused to use the word kidnapping, and his brain shut down the idea that Roddy had been murdered. "Haversham plans to use him for leverage."

"You believe your cover has been discovered?"

"I have no reason to believe it. But several days after Roddy came to see me at Haversham's, he disappeared. He received a note supposedly coming from me, asking him to come immediately to the club. That I was in dire need of his assistance. And Tessa overheard Yardley tell him when he arrived that I was upstairs with Haversham. Did Petersen report anything about Roddy's presence?"

"He didn't, but he wouldn't have any reason. Many gentlemen come to the club." Rathbourne leaned back in his chair and rubbed his chin. "Why kidnap Clifton now? If they wanted information about the treaty, why wait? We're missing something."

"It is hard to accept that Haversham was willing to risk his entire network to kidnap a titled earl and well-respected diplomat."

"He discovered your cover and wants revenge?" Rathbourne asked.

Dash shook his head. "I would expect Haversham to kill me in an alley with no way to tie him to the murder. He hasn't survived playing the middleman between the French and peers by taking chances."

"If the money from the French was big enough... what if one of his backers wants a bigger payout?" Rathbourne stood and walked to the window to gaze outside.

"We haven't proven that Weber, the biggest benefactor of the club, is part of the blackmailing ring. He is a slippery bastard. We know he had ties to criminal gangs throughout London."

Frustration poured through him. Dash shifted in the chair, needing to pace, to move.

Rathbourne had decided not to break up the network but, instead, to use Dash to spread disinformation to peers who were being blackmailed. The goal was to destroy any other French networks in London and their leader. This was the beginning of Dash and his team's work of discovering the next peer and inserting false documents.

"If it isn't my connection to Haversham, then it is Clifton's work with Hawkesbury. Vinson shared that Clifton and Pitt have been often seen at their club," Dash added.

"I'll go to Hawkesbury. He will confide in me. You must find Pitt and emphasize the importance of any information that can shed light on Clifton's disappearance. If you must, you can reveal our association but not your undercover work."

Dash's plan to return to Perdita's bedside vanished. But finding Roddy took priority, and Pitt had many connections and associations that could be helpful. Dash would have to wait to propose to

Perdita. Her business of helping spies was a stumbling block to his plan. Perdita wouldn't be easily convinced. She was a stubborn woman. He would have to keep her too busy in his bed and in his life for her to want to be involved in the war. Though, who was he kidding? Perdita wouldn't be deterred from taking action. She was a fighter and wouldn't give up what she believed. And that was one of the many reasons he loved her. He'd have to spend a very enjoyable lifetime negotiating with her. Heat spread through his body at the way he would convince Perdita to his way of thinking. And all the ways in which she would convince him.

Chapter Fifteen

DASH'S HEART THRASHED against his chest as if he had spent a round at Gleason's boxing club as he ascended the steps to Clifton house. He had been waiting for this moment for three long, lonely years. It was time to claim Perdita. He had done the honorable thing by walking away, but he no longer had to think of protecting her from scandal or his estate and the people who relied on him. She belonged with him. And he had been a fool to think he could survive without her. He could now provide a secure future for her. And make her happy.

Although it was now past eleven p.m., he couldn't wait to share the news of Roddy. Anything that would alleviate some of her worries. He felt hopeful for the first time, and nothing would stop him from being near Perdita.

After speaking with Rathbourne, he had met with Pitt, which took much longer than he had intended. It had taken hours to find the man. Dash then had to return to Rathbourne to share the important intelligence that Roddy was involved in espionage.

Pitt had been reticent to share the plan to have Napoleon assassinated by French royalists. Once Dash had the motive for Roddy's kidnapping, it gave focus to Rathbourne's men's search. It would only be a matter of time before they would find him. And then Dash could plan his future with Perdita. He would never expect her to wed without Roddy at her side.

Reese, a gigantic man with black hair and eyes, was at his post at the front door. Dash paused at the top of the outside steps, searching for the men he had assigned to guard the house. Dash spotted his man rounding the corner on his night watch. There were now three men who patrolled the grounds in shifts. All was in order. For the first time in days, the tightness in his chest had dissipated.

"Good evening, my lord." Reese stepped aside to allow Dash's entry. Reese's manner of speech never betrayed his Welsh roots.

"I would like to speak with Lady Perdita. It is important. I assume you would have notified me if there was any concern." Dash had instructed both Reese and Dr. Needham to send for him immediately with any change in Perdita's health.

"Of course, my lord. I understood your instructions. Lady Perdita should be home soon if you want to wait in the library. Is there anything I can get you while you wait?"

Red spots burst in front of Dash's eyes as his muscles clenched into fighting mode. Perdita, with a head injury and bruised ribs, had gone out after last night's assault. What danger was she pursuing while he believed she was resting at home? He had instructed the guards not to allow anyone onto the estate, but he hadn't considered he should have instructed them not to allow Perdita to leave. Harry wouldn't have allowed her to go anywhere without him.

Reese stepped back, sensing the outburst about to spew from Dash's mouth.

Dash swallowed hard against directing the anger at the butler, who had always welcomed and treated him as part of the family since the first time Dash came home from Eton with Roddy. But Dash couldn't stop the furious flush creeping up his collar into his face as he tried to contain his escalating exasperation. He liked order and for people to remain where he expected them to be.

"Perchance, can you explain to me what was of such import that the lady whom I left under a doctor's care needed to attend?"

"Lady Perdita slept all day, my lord, and rose quite restored. She has always been quick to recover from her injuries. She has a very strong constitution. Even as a girl, she never…"

Dash took one breath and then another. He was convinced steam must be blowing out of his ears. He spoke slowly and clearly. "Reese, where did she go?"

"She and Miss Rothsby are attending Lady Rathbourne's soiree. The event is to benefit the French emigres. Lady Perdita and Lady Rathbourne have formed a bond over their mutual French heritage. Lady Perdita has always had a soft spot for the poor French souls who fled during the scourge and now those who are fleeing Napoleon's tyranny. The event is very important to Lady Perdita."

Perdita's French grandmere was one of the souls who had to flee and resided with the family when Perdita was a young girl. Her husband wasn't as lucky to escape. As young children, Perdita and Roddy received affection and care from their grandmere in place of their absent parents. It was a huge loss for brother and sister when they were left with no one. Dash's mother had died during childbirth, so he never grieved as Roddy and Perdita had since he didn't know what he had missed. And his stepmother was not the nurturing type and might be part of the reason she never conceived the spare heir. She had tried to seduce him when he was fifteen years old. He had pensioned her off to Scotland, never to return once he assumed the title.

"Yes, of course. I know how generous Lady Perdita is." She always had a soft spot for the wounded. He was the perfect example of her need to rescue any suffering human or animal. He shouldn't be surprised by her charitable work or that she was friends with

Rathbourne's wife. What had Rathbourne said when Dash was leaving tonight? "If you love someone, you'll do anything, sacrifice anything to make them happy."

Dash wanted to spend his life making her happy. Just not allow her to take dangerous risks by being involved with covert work. Now that he thought about it, the school was a perfect solution for Perdita's need to be involved in the war effort. She could train others and oversee rather than put herself in jeopardy.

"She was feeling well enough to attend?" He had seen the carriages arriving at the Rathbourne estate, but he was focused on reporting his findings and not the evening's social events. Dash considered for a brief moment whether to ride back to Rathbourne's estate in search of Perdita. He was exhausted from traversing London in search of Pitt and was in no mood to share Perdita with society. He wanted to be alone with her.

"Yes. She was in good spirits." Reese escorted Dash to the library. "Would you like a tray, my lord? I know you've had a very demanding day."

"Thank you, Reese. I just realized I haven't eaten much today." He had been in a rush to get back to Perdita.

Dash ate the hearty fare that Totty had prepared with a snifter of brandy and then leaned back against the settee and closed his eyes for a brief respite.

He bolted awake at the sound of the door opening and the quiet *shush* of fabric along the wood floor.

Perdita had returned from her soiree and was moving across the room. "I'm sorry to awaken you. But Reese said you have important news."

He stood, tugging at his waistcoat, and ran his hand through his disheveled hair from today's heavy demands. He searched her face for signs of exhaustion or the aftereffects of her combat in the stables.

She showed no consequences of fending off two boxers with a pitchfork. She in fact looked more lovely in tonight's fashion. Her curls, except for a few wisps on her forehead and cheeks, were tucked into a blue turban, most likely to hide her scalp wound. The turban showcased her large and luminescent eyes shining as blue as the pendant from her grandmother, which rested on her glowing skin.

"I apologize. I must have drifted off waiting for you."

"You haven't slept since Haversham's have you?" With her radiant warmth directed at him, the coldness of the years melted away. It was a beautiful flashback of what his life had been like with Perdita. And what his future held.

"I'm sorry to have made you wait." She sat on a chair across from him, wincing when she attempted to reposition the pillow.

"You should be in your bed recovering. Not gallivanting around London." He immediately regretted the words but couldn't take them back. He forced his voice into a pleasant tone. "Reese explained about tonight's soiree. I know how much the cause means to you."

"You do?" Surprise widened her eyes.

"I never met your grandmere, but I know how important she was to you and Roddy." Dash lowered himself to the settee, wishing she were closer so he could take her into his arms and wipe away the sadness that crossed her face at the mention of her grandmere.

"What news of Roddy?" She looked down at her lap, away from his gaze.

How thoughtless of him not to speak of Roddy right away. Perdita was the only woman who caused him to lose his concentration by her mere presence.

"We haven't found him yet. But we will soon. I spoke with Pitt, and we have the motive, which will lead us to the kidnappers."

She twisted her hands together. "I don't understand."

"What I'm about to tell you, you must never confide to anyone, including Miss Rothsby. It is imperative for Roddy and our country's safety."

"He is on a secret mission?" Her voice lifted. "This is good news."

"Roddy was involved in a covert operation when he was in France. Pitt and his supporters funded French royalists to remove Napoleon and return the monarchy to France. Roddy brought the funds to France to give to the lords who want to overthrow Napoleon."

Dash didn't share that Yardley was part of the group to fund the assassination. He didn't want Perdita to take it upon herself to pursue Yardley after hearing that she and Miss Rothsby had been investigating him. Dash also didn't mention that Pitt and his secret committee hadn't shared the plan with Rathbourne, who was livid at the covert operation. Pitt's reasoning was that it gave them deniability during the peace treaty negotiations. The truth was that Pitt didn't want a veto or interference from the intelligence community. On hearing the news of Roddy's disappearance, Pitt became very forthcoming.

Pitt's man who orchestrated the exchange was captured by Fouche's secret police and tortured. It didn't take a highly trained operative to conclude that Napoleon wanted the names of his French enemies to eliminate them. Napoleon and Fouche excelled at getting rid of the little general's enemies. So much for the *liberte* for France.

"Roddy was kidnapped to identify the French lords who plotted against Napoleon?" All color left her face. "Roddy will never give them the names." Her quivering lips were pale.

"Perdita, let me hold you. I can't see you like this." Dash jumped from the settee.

She shook her head and put her hands up to stop him. "I'm fine. What is to be done?"

He didn't want to leave her but couldn't go against her wishes. He sat nearer to her.

"Rathbourne is using every resource to search for him. His men are reaching out to the underground connections and their informants. We know that Haversham has a smuggling operation down on the docks. Rathbourne's men are tearing the docks apart to find Roddy. Someone will have either seen or heard about Roddy. We will find him."

"Dash, be honest with me." He rejoiced at the use of his name on her lips, but it was for the wrong and awful reason. "Do you think they've already killed Roddy?" She stared at him, searching his face. The vulnerability in her eyes and voice was more excruciating agony than any stab wound that he had received.

He knelt next to her, taking her cold hand in his. "I am sure that Roddy is alive." He didn't know for how long, once they were able to get the information from him. Roddy was strong, but no man could withstand the torture forever. Fouche and his secret police were known for their brutal techniques.

"Thank you. But I know once they have the information, they'll have no reason to keep him alive."

So much for protecting Perdita from the harsh reality. "Yes, except I don't believe anyone who is helping the French would kill a titled peer. It will bring too much scrutiny to their illegal and treasonous activities. I will never stop hunting them. Nor will

Rathbourne."

"You speak of Haversham and his associates."

"Haversham is a broker and a businessman. He doesn't have loyalty to either side. He only seeks a profit. He has many avenues for making money, including blackmailing peers with their gambling debts to turn over state secrets to sell to the French. As you and Miss Rothsby have discovered about Yardley. And assisting in Roddy's disappearance smells of Haversham and his foul gang."

"You know of our work. Our plan?" She tried to pull her hand away, but he wasn't willing to release her now that he had her. He smoothed his thumb over her palm.

"Lord Rathbourne shared that you wanted to prove that women are capable of intelligence work. He is very impressed with your methods of gathering data. Not that I was surprised. You've always been an incredible woman, Perdita." Dash chose not to mention his initial reaction to the idea.

Her mouth opened and closed, and it would be so easy to lean in and take her lips. But not yet. Not until he'd made things right with her. He had a lot of groveling and begging ahead.

"Why would he reveal our plan for a school for women to you?" Her surprised response made it clear that she didn't hold him in the highest regard.

"He didn't mention the school precisely. But I can see how it would appeal to you."

Dash and Roddy had been shocked when Perdita, who wasn't interested in a lady's conduct, flourished at the finishing school. Perdita and a lady's finishing school were an oxymoron. She had developed friendships with the other young women, which had been missing in her life. "You would teach women self-defense and horsemanship? And Miss Rothsby would be part of this school too?"

Dash had already calculated that a school wouldn't put Perdita in direct danger. He could support the idea of the school. He had conditions for her involvement, but he would negotiate when she was his wife and in his bed.

"What is your relationship with Lord Rathbourne?" He hated how suspicious she was of him, as if he were the gambler and drunk he portrayed. Buried deep, he had nurtured the hope that Perdita wouldn't believe the rumors. That she would know he was better than his father.

"I've been working for over two years on his predecessor's request, investigating indebted peers who are selling secrets to Haversham. I've been posing as a drunk and a gambler to gather information to entrap Haversham."

Her wide eyes registered the shock, and her lips pursed in concentration. He smiled at the image of her mind whizzing like an automaton as she tried to make sense of the revelation.

"Yardley was our main focus at the beginning." When Dash was recruited, he was tasked with detecting Haversham's methods of targeting peers and how deep his network was.

"So, we were right." She grinned, lighting up the room with her glee. "Yardley is a traitor?"

"Yes. In his position on the military committee, Yardley is privy to all the country's planned expenditures, including the military budget and the intelligence budget. After hours of examining every one of Yardley's movements, we finally figured out how he passed the information. Yardley goes to the docks with his man of business each month to oversee the shipments from his holdings in the colonies. He leaves coded documents in the office to be picked up at a later date by Haversham's men."

"So why is Yardley still free? Why isn't he in prison?" Her forehead was crinkled in concentration.

He had to stop himself from kissing away her concerns. "We monitor what documents Yardley has access to and then we alter them and feed Yardley disinformation."

"That is brilliant." She clasped her hands together. "Yardley goes his merry way, thinking he is paying off his debts to Haversham, but he is paying with lies from us. And Haversham gives the French wrong information. It must be very difficult to decide on the information you share to keep the French from not becoming suspicious."

He had imagined this moment so many times when he came to her to finally tell her that he wasn't the man he presented himself to be. But never had he envisioned Perdita's excitement for the spy game or her immediate grasp of the difficulty of managing the intelligence to be fed to the French. Dash excelled at the logistical challenge with a range of variabilities to predict the most likely outcomes. He waged a silent battle against worthy foes. Brilliant Talleyrand and Fouche had been at the game a lot longer than Dash, which made his work all more demanding and intriguing.

"Dash, you've been doing honorable work all this time when I thought the worst of you. You allowed society to think it too."

The tenderness in the way she looked at him and the change in her voice was his undoing. Emotions clogged his throat, making it hard to speak. "It is an incredible relief to finally share that my life has been a lie."

"You aren't addicted to gambling?" She focused on his face. "You don't spend your nights in brothels? That woman I saw you with at Haversham's?"

"She is an informant who works for me. Nothing else ever happened between us."

"You were very convincing." The tenderness in her voice vanished. "And all the other women? Lady Marrowstone? Lady Wigley?"

He never blushed, but he felt heat rising to his face. How to account to Perdita of his destructive binge of sex and alcohol when he thought she was lost to him. "It was not well done of me. When I thought there was no hope between us, I went a little crazy. It didn't last long, and I regret every minute that I wasted trying to forget you, forget the future we planned."

"Why didn't you tell me? I would have kept your work a secret."

"Darling, can you please come and sit on the settee? This position is not conducive to what I have to say." And he needed access to kiss and touch her.

He offered his hand to help her rise. She placed her delicate hand in his. The frisson of her touch heated his blood and hardened his body instantaneously.

Distracted by her thoughts, she didn't show any awareness of his blistering need as she stood and reseated herself at one end of the settee. She didn't react when he sat close, with his hip and leg touching hers. "It is difficult to accept after the years of believing that you were going down the wrong path."

"After my father died, I was flailing because I had lost you and the future that I thought was mine. Sir Ramsey, the previous head of intelligence, approached me when I was regaining my fortune back at Haversham's. And instead of taking my gains and becoming a stodgy earl, I've allowed everyone to believe I'm a degenerate. But no longer. I've wanted to come to you so often, but my role required utter secrecy. And still requires it."

Dash had prepared this speech since Ramsey had asked him to work for him. Wanting her to see him as noble and self-sacrificing for the wellbeing of his country, he suddenly felt unsure. He had caused pain and mistrust between them that would take time to heal. Now with Roddy missing, she had to understand and accept the past belonged in the past because there was a chance that she was alone without anyone to protect her.

"Because I can go no longer without you in my life." Forget all his noble posturing. This was Perdita. "I've regretted the day I walked away from you… from us." He took her hand and pressed a kiss to her palm.

"Why would Lord Rathbourne allow you to share your role with me now?" Her face flushed as she chewed on her lower lip. Perdita wouldn't be deterred without answers.

"I told Lord Rathbourne that I planned to marry you, and I couldn't begin our marriage with a lie."

Dash couldn't stop touching her when she didn't offer any resistance. He explored the tender skin under the cap sleeve of her dress. Her breath hitched and her skin heated. The memory of how responsive she had been to his touch fueled his growing hunger. "You understand the sensitivity of the work with your information gathering. Speaking of sensitivity…" He used his finger to trace her beating pulse on her graceful neck before he lowered and used his tongue, watching as her pulse sped and color covered her cheeks.

"Secondly, you deserve information about the reason for Roddy's disappearance since Haversham and Yardley are involved." He leaned close and whispered into her ear, surprised at how his voice came out more like a growl.

"This is all hard to grasp." Her voice was husky and breathless. And he ignored the need to joke about how he wanted her to grasp something harder.

He took her face between his hands and stared into her eyes.

Wanting to feel the soulful connection that he hungered for. "And thirdly, because I want to marry you. I can't go on in this world without you by my side. I don't want long nights alone. I never want to go to bed without you. I want to be the man who you tangle with in silky sheets. I want to be the man whose name you call out in surrender. Marry me, my darling. I love you and always will, always have. Let me be the center of your life. I promise to make you the center of mine. I will always be true and work never to disappoint you."

Tears welled in her eyes. She touched his face with gentleness, her eyes filled with love. "Dash, I feel like I'm in a dream. It is more fantastical than I could have ever imagined. I did imagine many scenarios when you came back and begged my forgiveness."

"I'm here begging your forgiveness. Please, Perdita. I'll get down on my knees and beg. You don't have to say yes now. I will wait. I've already waited so long. What are a few more days?"

"Days? Are you insane?"

Her mouth opened in surprise, making it too difficult to resist. He had planned to be gentle, but feeling the press of her soft, warm lips against his ignited all his suppressed needs. He devoured her mouth, sucking her lower lip, outlining the seams with his tongue before he pressed into her mouth. His tongue darting in and out and dueling with Perdita just as though they had never left off. The taste of her sweet lips filled a void in his soul. He couldn't stop kissing her.

"Darling, invite me to your bedroom." He gasped between kissing the sensitive spot below her ear that always drove her crazy.

She stiffened in his arms before pulling away. "Is that how it is done? I'm to invite you?"

He wanted to laugh and kiss her senseless all at the same time.

"You silly goose. I want to make love to you, but I don't want Reese or Totty to find us. They are like your parents."

Then the woman he loved laughed. "Do you think Reese would challenge you to a duel?"

And suddenly the joking was gone since Roddy, if he were here, would possibly challenge him to a duel.

"Dash, I can't do any of this…" She gestured to encompass them. "Roddy is missing. Right now, finding him is all that matters. And I need time to adjust to everything you've shared. I spent years thinking the worst of you." She gave him a rueful half smile.

"We can wait. I'm a patient man." Kissing his way up her arm, he nuzzled her neck, causing her to shiver.

She giggled. "You are not a patient man. Unless you've changed radically."

"Darling, I'm a new man with you back in my life. A paragon of virtue." He teased her nipple feeling it harden under his touch.

A flush spread across her chest as she leaned forward to give him more access. His self-restraint wavered with her moan.

"This is torture, darling." His hands shook with the effort to pull away from her. "We must stop." Speaking aloud helped him gain some semblance of control over the lustful fog blocking all rational thought. Every cell in his being cried out to take her, claim her as his. His logical self roused enough to know Perdita would regret a fast coupling in the library. When they came together, he wanted no regrets, no guilt, only pure pleasure and love.

He kissed her gently, taking time to rub his lips against hers. "We will wait until Roddy is returned." He placed kisses on her nose, her eyelids, and then her lips. "And then I'm taking you to bed and never letting you leave."

Chapter Sixteen

P ERDITA DIDN'T WANT her dream to end. It was perfect. Dash was perfect. Nothing could hurt her again. Dash lifted her into his strong arms as he whispered that he had waited for her forever, and he would go slow. She didn't want slow. She wanted everything his gravelly voice promised. Drifting in and out of hazy light, she swayed back and forth, reveling in the sensation of Dash's closeness and his soothing tone.

Panic replaced her sensual feelings as she was dragged from Dash, from safety into a terrifying nightmare. Bony fingers squeezed her so tightly that she couldn't breathe. She was lost on a cliff unable to get her bearings. Each step along the steep incline was grueling and precarious on the wet slippery ground. She was desperate to find someone, but she didn't know who she sought. The air reeked of spoiled fish. She looked down at the abrupt drop into the water. An eerie black nothingness.

Terror of falling into the void engulfed her. The only sound was her pounding heartbeat. She shouted for Dash, but nothing came out of her mouth. She stumbled and was swept into the waves, the strong current taking her down, shrouded by the arctic water into the silent, black emptiness.

Perdita awoke to the sound of men shouting. She wanted to pull the pillow over her head to stop the loud noise. Her servants would never disturb her. Where was Rosetta with her morning chocolate?

The deafening clamor was unbearable. The mention of Dash's name in the tirade drew her attention. Blinking, she pushed her eyes open to come awake, fighting against the heaviness weighing her limbs and eyelids, and sat up.

She lifted her hand to cover her mouth to stop herself from vomiting as stabbing pain twisted behind her eyes. Her hand didn't budge. It took a few seconds for her lethargic brain to register the fact that her hands were bound with rough rope, bringing back the memory of two men climbing into her carriage. Rough cruel men with their weapons pointed at her heart entered from each side when the carriage abruptly halted in the middle of the road. The shock of the boldness of their attack in midday on her way to visit Aunt Euphemia had slowed her reaction to fight back.

She had raised her arm to knock the pistol out of the man's arm, planning to kick the other man's pistol. It had been too difficult to maneuver in the small space against the two armed opponents. Her kidnapping had been carefully and perfectly executed, leaving her with no defense.

The voices outside the room grew louder.

"I'm not hanging for your bloody ass and your Frenchie friends. I never agreed to this. Beldon will come after us for touching the woman. He has been friends with Clifton and his sister for years. He attended her ball. If rumors are to be believed, he plans to marry her."

"You were very happy to take the Frenchie's money. And Beldon will never find them."

"You underestimate him."

"He's a drunk who does nothing but drink, gamble, and whore just like his father. We had men follow him for weeks when you were convinced he was working for Rathbourne. And that led nowhere."

"It won't be just Beldon. The entire country will want our blood if we kill an earl and his sister."

Terror clambered through her sluggish brain, bolting her wide awake. The good news was that Roddy must still be alive, wasn't it? Disoriented and dizzy, she searched for the voices coming from above who spoke easily about murdering her and Roddy. Moving her head caused the piercing pain to shoot straight to her brain, and another wave of nausea to roll over her.

An open porthole above her allowed the men's voices to be heard and morning light to filter into the area. How long had she been unconscious? The memory of the kidnapper striking her with the butt of his pistol as the other grabbed her arms flashed before her.

One of the men speaking must be Haversham, who ran his smuggling operation at Upper Pool docks if Harry's contact was correct.

But why would the club owner link himself to the kidnapping by summoning Roddy to his club with the fake note? Dash was convinced that Haversham's business savvy wouldn't let him be stupid enough to kill Roddy. But his secret partner seemed willing to kill them.

The Upper Pool docks were not far from Mayfair, on the Thames that stretched a little less than a mile below London Bridge. There were thousands of ships in the docks waiting to either have their cargo loaded or unloaded. How would Rathbourne's men find her and Roddy? They would have to go through the port records to find the names of ships that might be associated with Haversham. Unless they already knew the ships' names owned by Haversham, it would take hours or possibly days to locate them. Too long before…

she didn't finish the thought as the tiny hairs on her neck bristled in foreboding.

"It isn't Beldon that you should worry about. Fouche's secret agents are barbarians who enjoy watching people suffer. What do you think they'll do to you if we don't finish this?" This man didn't speak like a gentleman, which ruled out Yardley or Vinson as Haversham's co-conspirator.

"You got us into this mess. If the French or Beldon don't kill you, then I'm going to tear you apart." With Haversham's violent background, he most likely was the one speaking.

"Then I'll hope for Beldon. I've watched you in the ring." The man's deep laugh boomed. Who was able to laugh at dying? Perdita gulped down the anxiety the size of a boulder stuck in her throat. Only someone with nothing to lose.

"If we don't get the names from Clifton, Fouche's men will dole out our slow and painful deaths." Haversham sounded afraid, which heightened her own torment.

She held herself still, fighting against the panic. These villains frightened a man who had made his living beating others to an inch of their lives.

"Something to look forward to—watching you suffer at your supposed friends' hands."

"Why all this drama, Haversham? We've been in tighter spots. Clifton will give up the names when we threaten to rape his sister. And then we'll be done."

"You're a bigger fool than I thought if you think we can walk away from this."

"You've always hated those titled bastards. You would have been amused that the men all want a chance at having a lady, an earl's sister."

Perdita began to shake. Whole-body tremors took over. Her teeth clacked and the smell of saltwater filled her nostrils and made her gag. What names did Roddy possess that made them desperate?

She lowered her head onto her chest to stop the wave of dizziness and to block out the ship rocking. The pendant from grandmere was still fastened around her neck. She touched her most prized possession and felt the courage the simple necklace represented. She could find the strength against all odds as her grandmere had done. She was Annette's granddaughter with a heritage to honor.

"Let's get a drink before the French arrive. It will help us."

They were leaving… for now. She jerked her head fast, bringing a jolt of agony. She had to find Roddy. She could barely see in the dim space filled with stacked boxes. She had to free her hands, find Roddy, and escape before the men returned. The sound of rats scurrying sent a chill through her trembling body.

Hyperalert to every sound—lapping water, caw of seagulls, the scuffle of feet, and distant shouts—she waited for anything to help get her bearing. The ship wasn't sailing yet, which made their chances of escaping better. But how long before they voyaged away from London and away from Dash? She had no doubt he was searching right now. He would be raging as was his way when he was frightened and alone. Anger was always his first form of protection, learning early to fight back against his drunken father.

A surge of energy shot through her; she wasn't going to allow these men to hurt Dash or Roddy. Both men would be devastated if anything happened to her. She finally had a future with Dash, and nothing would stop her from escaping.

Her heartbeat sped, her muscles tightened, and her mind focused. Was Roddy being held in a different area of the cargo hold? As her eyes adjusted to the light, she pushed herself from the mat on the floor to stand. The men had been stupid not to tie her feet which could be used as lethal weapons. Of course, they didn't consider she had any chance of escaping from a ship. And most likely, they had men standing watch on the dock. She and Roddy were strong swimmers and wouldn't be deterred by the filthy river water if it meant evading rape and death.

She wobbled but was upright as another wave of dizziness struck. She took two steps to test her balance. She had to find a sharp edge to cut the ropes that were thick and tightly bound. It wouldn't be a quick job. The men's voices had drifted farther away from the porthole. How much time did she have before they returned with Fouche's men?

She moved quickly along the long rows of stacked wooden crates. Her eyes darted back and forth between the rows, alert to any sound of the return of her captors. She had to find a tool to cut the ropes, but so far, all she had found were stacks and stacks of closed crates, and the only other occupants were skittering rats. She was almost halfway across the expansive space when she found him.

Roddy lay on a mat a few feet from the wooden ladder that led out of the hold. He wasn't bound. His stillness disturbed her. She cautiously approached him, listening and looking for any sign of a guard. No one watched him probably because he was unconscious.

"Roddy," she whispered as she knelt next to him. "It's Dita. Dearest, wake up."

He didn't stir. A sob escaped before she covered her mouth with her forearm to stop the crashing grief at the sight of Roddy bruised and beaten. His blond curls were matted with blood, his face misshapen, and his mouth hung open with blood dried on his lips. His eyes were swollen shut. Blood dripped from a long slash across his cheek.

Terror crushed her ability to draw air. Had the men already killed her brother? She watched Roddy's chest, her heart lodged in the throat waiting for a sign of life. After what felt like an eternity, relief surged through her at the sight of his slow breath.

She leaned closer to whisper in his ear. "Roddy, you must wake up."

Roddy didn't respond, so she nudged his arm with her bound hands. "It's Dita. You must try to open your eyes. I know you're in pain..." She swallowed the whimper. "Please, Roddy, open your eyes for me."

"Are you real?" His rusty voice was barely audible.

"Dearest, I'm real. And we're leaving this ship. I need to find something to cut my ropes. We must go before the men come back."

"Leave me. I can't make it." He shook his head. "Dash has always loved you. Marry him."

"You're an arse to think I'd leave you. We've been in sticky situations before." She tried for a humorous tone before she wept aloud.

"I'm sorry, Dita. So sorry that I got you into this."

"When this is over, you can apologize. I need something sharp. You rest, and once I have my hands free, we're leaving."

"Axes and hammers are hanging on the far side of the wall near the lamps and coal bucket. I haven't been able to make it there. But I've been planning..."

She followed Roddy's directions, moving swiftly. She could use all the tools as weapons once she got her hands free to fight. How many men guarded Roddy, and where were his jailors right now? She didn't know how long she had been unconscious to know the time of day. By the darkening light, it was sunset. What agony Dash must be suffering with her missing for so long.

She found the area that Roddy described. She debated whether to knock off the large, serrated knife hanging by its handle on the wall. The heavy working blade would make a loud sound when it fell and possibly alert the guards. But what other choice did she have? She had to have her hands free to fight back. Using her bound hands, she whacked the serrated knife to the floor and then waited in endless silence to be found.

Dropping to the ground, she maneuvered the knife between her legs, then began to push the rope back and forth on the knife. The tension on the rope burned her wrists. It felt like it took an eternity to break through the rope, with her heart speeding and an anxious awareness of every sound, waiting for her captors.

She shook her hands to bring the blood flow back once the rope unraveled. She gathered an ax, two knives, and a hammer to arm her and Roddy. She was tucking a knife into her petticoats when she heard voices. Two distinct voices. She waited, listening for any others. Darn, darn. She hadn't time to concoct the plan to escape. Her mind focused on how to take on the two men in the hold without alerting anyone else.

Quickly she ran through possible scenarios before coming to what might work. *Might* being the operative word. She slashed her skirt with the sharp knife, tearing away most of her favorite flowered muslin, leaving only the bodice intact. She needed her legs to be free to defend herself. The skirt hung in tatters. Her undergarment didn't provide any manner of propriety and didn't conceal the knife. Desperate times warranted desperate actions. Then she prayed that her disheveled state and revealing appearance would be a distraction.

She held the ax and the hammer behind her back, placing the second knife on the floor. She staggered out from behind the stacks and whispered in a stage voice, "Help me. Please can someone help me?"

Chapter Seventeen

DASH AND JONES stared down at the bloated body of Yardley floating in the Thames. Yardley's eyes were open, and his face contorted in an unworldly and ghoulish manner. Yardley deserved his watery grave, but Dash wouldn't forget the appalling sight for a long time.

Dash should have remained in his office, looking at the ship manifests, but frustration pushed him to get out of his office and into the field. He had decided to help in the search for Roddy on the Upper Pool docks. Dash needed some action before he had to spend another long night at Haversham's while controlling the urges not to beat Roddy's whereabouts out of the boxer. Controlling his urges wasn't his strong point lately. Not since the reappearance of Perdita in his life. Everything was more vivid, more alive, and possible. But underlying fears plagued him, warning that happiness could disappear as it had upon his father's death.

He had been a saint last night, and he was paying the price. He was tense and irritable, and all he could think about was making Perdita his. He had been pleasuring himself with Perdita fantasies all these years apart. But solo acts could no longer bring satisfaction when he'd had the living sensual woman in his arms, ripe for seduction.

"Beldon, I'll alert the other men. Do you want to wait and see the cause of death?" Jones asked.

Snapped out of his pleasurable reverie, Dash shook his head. "No, Haversham or his boss is getting desperate and cleaning up messes." Saying it aloud, Dash felt a frisson of foreboding. Had they killed Roddy? He suddenly needed to see Perdita and reassure himself that she was safe. Today was Wednesday, and the day she spent the afternoon with Aunt Euphemia. The two women had become fast friends. Everyone loved Perdita. He was one damn fortunate man that she was forgiving. He wasn't sure he could say the same about himself. If Perdita ever betrayed him, he didn't want to think of his reaction. Still, he knew once she gave her heart that she would hold steadfast. It eased his mind.

The discovery of Yardley's body was a very good reason to appear at Rathbourne House and discuss the meaning behind the murder of a respected titled peer. Their theory that Haversham would never risk the murder of a peer was wrong. What else had they gotten wrong? His fear for Roddy bourgeoned, and with it, his unease about Perdita. Had Yardley been killed because Haversham's French connection had discovered that the documents were doctored? But how did it connect to Roddy and his involvement in the plot to assassinate Napoleon? If they only knew what Yardley had taken out of Roddy's library.

"Have the men dredge the river for other bodies." Dash's voice almost broke. They had to search. He refused to consider that Roddy's body was in the Thames, and what it would mean to Perdita if her brother had been murdered. He suddenly needed to hold Perdita, to reassure her that everything would be fine. Maybe he'd convince himself as well.

"We should pay Vinson a visit. The shock of hearing that his friend was found floating in the Thames may be enlightening." Dash would have to wait for his reunion with Perdita.

"Let me deliver the news. I won't mince any words like a gentleman would. And you can be the sympathetic friend and peer." The glee in Jones's voice was amusing at this low point.

"Good idea. You can ask the unseemly questions about Yardley's gambling debts and links to Haversham that aren't allowed by a gentleman. And if that doesn't rattle Vinson, I'll mention the rumors that Haversham blackmails his gamblers."

"I'm going to enjoy this."

Dash couldn't help but chuckle at the reticent soldier's wide grin, knowing his chance to see Perdita this afternoon was gone. She was attending the opera tonight with Aunt Euphemia and Miss Rothsby. Hopefully, he'd be able to arrive when the opera was finished to escort the ladies home.

"Let's head to White's. If my sources are correct, he spends his afternoons there."

"Have you wondered why Vinson wasn't blackmailed by Haversham?"

"We've had this discussion. There is no evidence that he is being blackmailed. Vinson doesn't serve on any committees that Haversham or the French must feel are of any importance. Or that has been our working assumption."

After hours of wasted time trying to find Vinson with no success, Dash was on his way to discuss Yardley's death and Vinson's disappearance with Rathbourne. Neither Vinson's butler nor his man of business could shed any light on where his lordship was. It was highly suspect. Rathbourne would need to use part of his manpower to search for Vinson unless his body had been found in the Thames too.

Dash jumped out of his carriage at Rathbourne House, noting the Clifton carriage on the drive, which was surprising. It was late for Perdita to still be visiting and too early to depart for the opera. Despite the long and frustrating day, happiness flooded him at the chance to see Perdita. He never was happy. Not without Perdita.

He didn't see Harry, who was in charge of Perdita's movement. And Dash's man, a seasoned soldier, rode postillion. He was smarter now in dealing with Perdita. He didn't demand she stay home, but he could make certain that she was well protected.

The door was opened by Brompton, a stoic quiet man, who, with his outgoing wife, was in charge of one of the most important households in all of England.

"Thank heavens you've arrived. Men have been searching for you for hours…"

Had he entered another realm? A verbose Brompton breaking all butler protocols was enough to make a man unsteady. And then fear gut punched him, making it hard not to bend over from the blow. Roddy's body was found, and Perdita had learned the news and had come to Aunt Euphemia for comfort. "What's happened?"

Brompton stiffened. "My deepest apologies, my lord, for my outburst. It is just that we all have become attached to Lady Perdita, and the idea that someone would want to harm her…"

Dash staggered, using the door jamb for support from the crushing body blow as the words replayed. Perdita and harm. "Tell me."

Everything faded; the lights dimmed. He wasn't aware that he had shouted, but by the sudden appearance of Rathbourne at his side, he must have.

"Steady, man. We'll find her."

And his knees buckled and his stomach lurched. He stumbled before he felt Rathbourne's hand at his elbow. "Let's get you a drink. You've had a shock."

Dash pulled away. "Don't mollycoddle me, Rathbourne."

He followed Rathbourne into his office. His mind was swirling but not in any cohesive manner.

Miss Rothsby stood in the middle of the room, her shoulders hunched as she wept into a handkerchief. And upon seeing him, she rushed toward him and threw herself against him. "You must find her. It's all my fault. I encouraged her to be a spy. We thought we were so clever."

Dash wrapped his arms around the small frame of the woman who had made her dislike for him obvious. He patted her on the back. Her distress helped him regain his composure. "Here, here now. We will find her. Lady Perdita is strong and smart and will fight." He wanted to believe every word.

Miss Rothsby snuffled and then pulled back, stepping out of his embrace. "I'm sorry, my lord. I'm not usually apt to lose my equanimity. But without Roddy to turn to…" Her voice broke, and she patted her eyes with the handkerchief stuffed into her hand.

"Please sit down and tell me everything." He led her to the settee. Dash was ready to decimate everything and everyone in his path, but taking it out on Perdita's closest and distressed friend was not an option.

"The carriage was set upon by four men. Harry was shot and your man was killed. Dita was forced into a waiting carriage by two men. It is all that Harry can remember. Harry was found bleeding in the street and taken into a home. He was unconscious, but when he woke, he immediately sent a message to Clifton house. I came here as soon as I could."

In broad daylight in the middle of London, Perdita had been taken with two of his best men guarding her. Haversham and his men were escalating. Yardley had been killed, Vinson was missing, and now Perdita. They were desperate.

Rathbourne handed him a brandy. "Drink this. I need you on top of the game."

Dash threw back the fine French cognac, feeling the smooth burn down his throat.

"Was there anything out of the ordinary in Lady Perdita's routine this morning?" Rathbourne sat across from Miss Rothsby. "Anything unusual?"

"Nothing. I barely spoke with her. She slept late, which was unusual, but she was in great spirits." Miss Rothsby blushed as she pushed her glasses on her nose.

"I asked Perdita to marry me last night." Dash looked at Rathbourne.

Whatever the man saw, he nodded in understanding. "When we have Lady Perdita back, I will share the perils my wife put me through. Women are stronger than we ever give them credit for."

Rathbourne's confidence and his steady voice calmed Dash enough that he could listen to Miss Rothsby. But they were wasting time. He had to get to Harry to learn if he had any clues to identify the men.

"You've sent a message to the men on the docks of Upper Pool to search for Lady Perdita? Someone must have seen them forcing a woman onto a ship in the middle of the day."

"Upper Pool docks?" Miss Rothsby interjected. "At last night's ball..." She pushed her glasses with one finger to right them. "You both are aware that Dita and I have been gathering information about Lord Yardley at society events. My role is to listen for gossip amongst the companions and dowagers and in the retiring room. I also am skilled at reading lips. Last night, Lord Vinson was speaking with Lord Yardley about Carolina, which caught my attention since Dita and I thought it was a woman's name when we first heard it.

We've been searching for connections. But he said something about Carolina and the West Indies docks. I cannot discern a great deal of the conversation by lip reading, but I can recognize distinct words and deduce meaning from the words and body language."

"Oh, my God. We've been searching at the wrong docks. I'm headed there now. And the Carolina must be a ship. Can you assemble the men I need?" Dash felt a flash of hope. Their first real clue.

"Very savvy to distract us to search Upper Pool docks with Haversham's smuggling enterprise located there." Rathbourne stood. "Wait, I'm going with you."

"But you… your identity will be…" Dash was already headed to the door.

"They already know who I am. And after the years of watching them, I want to face those slimy bastards for thinking they can take a lady off our streets."

"What should I do?" Miss Rothsby asked, her voice now clear.

"You must rest, my dear. Please ring the bell and have Mrs. Brompton bring you tea. I will inform you as soon as we have news."

Dash and Rathbourne rode in silence in the carriage. Dash had debated whether to have a horse saddled, but he was too impatient to get to the West Indies docks. The area was expansive, but now they had a name, the name he had found scribbled on a sheet of paper in Haversham's office. It wouldn't be like the search of Upper Pool where there were hundreds of ships and nothing to differentiate between them. They would find the dockmaster at West Indies, and he would direct him to the ship. And then he would obliterate everyone who was part of harming Perdita.

He focused on the details of his plan because if he didn't, he would sink into the darkness where primal panic lived. His life without Perdita was nothing. As children, she had filled the emptiness of his existence. He'd rather die than live in the world without her.

"I know that look. But you'll be of no use to Lady Perdita if you are not in control. She will need you to use all your wits."

What did Rathbourne know? He had a wonderful aunt and sister who adored him. Roddy and Perdita were his only family.

"Why take Lady Perdita? And why now?"

"You want to talk about this now?" Dash considered grabbing Rathbourne by the neck and choking him.

Rathbourne raised his eyebrow. The smug bastard.

"It must mean that Clifton is alive." Rathbourne leaned against the squab in Dash's carriage.

"Yes." A spark of hope flared in Dash's chest.

"Lady Perdita knows of Clifton's involvement in Pitt's scheme, but she has no useful information. They must plan to use her as leverage to make Clifton talk," Rathbourne said in his analytical voice. "She was taken four to five hours ago."

Dash's throat constricted, making it hard to get air into his lungs, at Rathbourne's careless description of brutal men using Perdita. "What the hell, Rathbourne? How is it helpful to know that they are threatening Lady Perdita?"

"Exactly. Threaten. Not harm her. But we must find her quick-ly."

And with that pithy comment, Dash's fear ricocheted off the walls. He had to get to her in time. She was well trained in defending herself. His need to be logical wasn't suppressing the entire body alarm. Perdita had only fought against Alfie, Harry, Roddy, and himself. All men who loved her and would never hurt her. It was all a game. She had never fought against deadly evil men who killed without blinking an eye. He prayed that she kept her bravery at the forefront of her mind. He prayed to the God he'd abandoned years before.

Chapter Eighteen

U SING THE ELEMENT of surprise by her rumpled and risqué appearance and her plea for help, Dita had struck one guard with the hammer, knocking him out, then swiveled and kicked the other in the groin, bringing him to his knees before she hit him with the hammer. A wild burst of energy exploded through her as she rushed to Roddy, darting between two unconscious men at her feet.

"My God, Dita, you were unstoppable with the hammer."

One good thing so far was that her defense had invigorated her brother. She didn't respond that the threat of rape and murder would give anyone the strength of Goliath. Amazing what vigor you could summon when you were fighting for your life.

"I wish Alfie could have seen you." Roddy was on all fours, pushing himself to stand.

She didn't tell Roddy that she had felt her grandmere's spirit before she confronted the men. It wasn't the time, and she didn't think Roddy would understand the connection between the women.

She rushed to help him, grabbing his elbow to steady him. "I was so afraid I would kill them, but the hammer is so heavy that a small arc was enough momentum to knock them out without delivering a mortal blow."

"You should not be worried about killing them. They planned to kill us."

She had to really think this killing business through at a later time. She didn't want to kill people even if they deserved it. Had Dash killed anyone? She couldn't think of Dash right now. He must be frantic and frightened and raging at everyone.

"We need to get out of here before anyone else comes. You're going to have to climb the ladder on your own."

Roddy leaned against her, giving her most of his weight. Moving slowly, he shuffled without enough strength or energy to lift his feet. With every ragged breath, Dita's panic heightened. If they didn't make it out of the hold, they would be trapped. And on discovering she had disarmed their men, she didn't want to consider the retribution the captors would deliver.

She had to keep her focus on leaving. *What-ifs* would not help anyone. At least the distance to the ladder wasn't far as she dragged Roddy to their only means of escape. The porthole wasn't large enough for them to use.

She stopped a few feet before the ladder and released Roddy. She raised her finger to her mouth for silence. Before ascending, she had to check whether anyone stood guard over the entrance to the hold. The view was clear from fifteen feet below. She counted at least twenty rungs that Roddy would have to climb. There was no other choice.

Roddy, standing behind her, whispered, "I should go first."

She faced him. "Roddy, this is not the time to be a gentleman. You do not have the strength to fight." She doubted he could make the climb, but if she was able to clear the deck, she could return and assist him.

"I'm not letting my sister sacrifice herself for my sake."

"This is not the time for chivalry. Do you want to stay alive and escape? My choice is to continue to live."

"Good point. I'm so sorry I got you into this mess."

"No apologies. Use your strength to get up the ladder. Rest after each rung." She hoped by the time Roddy reached the top, she would have freed the way. And if not, Roddy didn't need to suffer more.

She climbed quickly, grateful for not having much of her skirt to impede the climb. The hammer and knife were tucked into her petticoat. She had fashioned a belt from the skirt material to hold the hammer in place in back. She would use the short-hilted knife as a last resort. The hammer, with its long handle and weight, required a larger arc to swing and would give her the element of surprise. And it meant she didn't have to get as close to her opponent.

She amazed herself at the ease with which she ascended. How long would this surge of energy last before she wilted? Her heart sprinted, her vision narrowed, and she was ultra-focused on the next battle she faced. Could she train other women to act as fiercely when threatened?

Vulnerable the moment she climbed onto the deck, she paused three rungs below and listened to gauge how many men were present. There was the sound of seagulls, and men shouting in the distance but nothing close, no footsteps that she could discern. She steeled herself, trying to not think of Dash and the regret that they hadn't made love. If she and Roddy lived through this, she planned to take Dash to her bed and not allow him to leave.

She gingerly climbed, her heart pounding so loudly she was sure the men would hear her. With her head level with the deck, she slowly peered at the surrounding area, gazing up at the mast and the furled sails. She saw no one except one guard with a wiry frame and strong arms most likely from lifting crates. He was ten to twelve feet away, leaning over the railing to watch the dock's activities below the ship. He was stationed by the hole to prevent them from leaving and watching for anyone who approached. Or that was her conjecture.

She ducked her head back. Only three men—if she counted the two she had knocked unconscious—were guarding such high-value prisoners. But where were the other men?

And once she disarmed the guard, how would they get off without jumping into the water? Roddy was in no condition to swim. She had never been on a ship. She only knew about walking the plank from pirate stories… She and Roddy would be exposed if they ran down a plank. That was the next challenge.

The first was how to silence the man without killing him. She didn't want him to call out for reinforcements or alert the men on the dock. She'd have to use the hammer again and go for a head strike. She shuddered at the memory of the sensation of the hefty weight making contact with the other men's skulls. Both were breathing and would recover. Shooting them would have raised the risks of their discovery if she had a pistol, and most likely the men would have died from infection. She reassured herself that the hammer was more humane. She was stalling, steeling herself to hit someone who wasn't attacking her. The other men, once they realized her ruse, attempted to grab and punch her. It was easier to fight back than be the aggressor.

She reminded herself of the plans that the men had for her and Roddy. Taking a slow deep breath to center herself and her focus, she searched the area again. Only one man was visible. She could hear voices from the dock below but nothing else. She climbed onto the deck, searching in a full circle, then tiptoed with the hammer fisted behind her back. It was heavy and her arms ached.

She was within striking distance when he must have heard her approach. He spun as he reached for his pistol. His mouth opened, ready to shout when she reacted instinctually. She pivoted on her right foot, kicking the pistol out of his hand as she swung and hit him in the face with the hammer. Blood spurted out of his nose as he fell to the deck with a loud thud.

She turned three hundred sixty degrees to see whether the sound had alerted his fellow conspirators. Nothing. Twenty feet to the front of the ship was their escape—a wooden plank connecting to the dock. She would have to move Roddy into the open area, leaving them exposed.

She peered over the side of the boat, looking for more men guarding the plank. No one stood near the entry onto the ship. Men were pushing carts next to the horse-laden carts. If she could get Roddy on a cart, they could leave undetected. Her and Roddy's unkempt appearance would draw attention. She had considered removing one of the fallen men's breeches, but the idea of undressing was unsavory and would take too long. She was barely covered in her slashed skirts. The dock was teeming with men. A shiver coursed through her at the men's possible reactions to her risqué dress. And if that wasn't enough to make her falter, she was sure that Haversham's men were among the many on the dock.

What other choice did she have? There was no place to hide on the ship, and it might take days for Dash to find her. Days that Roddy didn't have.

She dashed to the ladder as Roddy climbed onto the deck. He was deathly pale, his eyes sunken in his skull, and his body trembling. He had used his last reserves of energy. It fell on her to get them off their prison.

She took his arm. She was a tall, strong woman who could possibly carry Roddy on her back, but it would leave them unprotected. She had to be able to react if confronted.

She took his arm and started the next part of their journey, pulling him into the open space. The exposure raised the hairs on the back of her neck; foreboding hovered as a silent specter. She had to shake off the surge of anxiety. She had to control her emotions. Hadn't Alfie taught her how to keep her focus?

The eerie silence broken only by the shuffle of Roddy's boots on the wood caused her heart to race and her muscles to clench in preparation.

They had made it more than halfway when men's voices echoed from the plank. Roddy, exhausted, didn't protest when she hauled him behind her. Yanking the hammer from her back, she gripped it tight. She readied for the next fight, blocking everything from her mind but protecting them. She had to win. She stepped forward to face her opponents.

"Dita, you're so damn brave," Roddy murmured.

She recognized both men who boarded the ship. It was Haversham and the heavy man she had seen when she was disguised as a servant. And behind them was a guard with a pistol leveled at her.

"My, my. What do we have here?" Haversham's partner moved in a slow, predatory manner, his eyes raking over her and stopping to stare at her most private areas. She pulled the scraps of material to hide herself.

He and Haversham laughed. The cruel sound enraged and terrorized her. Their black souls made her skin crawl. The triumph in their voices incensed her. She wanted to attack and wipe their smug, condescending grins off their faces for what they had done to Roddy.

"Haversham, this little lady has put your men to shame by her appearance with her brother on the deck. Lady Perdita, I assume." He bowed his head as if meeting in society.

She didn't answer, trying to think of an escape. She could hurt the fat one but likely would get shot in the process. Except they didn't want her dead since they needed Roddy's cooperation. She rolled onto her toes to at least cause damage when she heard Roddy's voice. "Don't, Dita. They'll only hurt you more."

"Perdita."

She quickly looked for the source of the illusion that sounded like Dash. With her entire focus on the men, she had missed other men boarding the ship. Dash, pistol in hand, flew toward her. He was followed by an armed Lord Rathbourne. A stream of soldiers with rifles rushed behind Lord Rathbourne as another group scrambled aboard from the waterside.

She had never seen the ferocious and feral look on Dash's face as he neared. He seemed to grow bigger as his vehemence fueled his body.

"My God, what have they done to you?" The agony in his voice was overwhelming. "Did they… ravish you?"

She was paralyzed in shock. Dash had come. Astonished that he had found her, she stared, trying to make sense of the rapid shift in their position.

"I'm going to rip you bastards apart. You'll beg like little boys to stop the agony." He roared and rushed Haversham. The violence in his voice chilled her.

A panicked Haversham reached to grab her arm, but she dodged him and was about to kick him when Dash inserted himself between them. He pulled her against him with his free hand. "No need, darling. I will destroy them."

In the seconds of the scuffle, Lord Rathbourne now stood behind Haversham with a pistol at his head. And at least twenty men pointed rifles at the three villains. The fat lecher had a gun at his temple too. The reality that she and Roddy were safe was beginning to sink in.

"Rathbourne, do not shoot Haversham. And Jones, don't you dare kill Weber. I have a hell planned for them for touching Perdita."

"Dash." She turned in his arms, needing to see his face, to look directly into his eyes. The heat of his rage blasted through her. "They didn't touch me in the way you mean. I did this to my skirts as a ruse to draw the guards close enough to strike them."

"They didn't?" His voice was hoarse, his eyes searching hers for reassurance.

"I'm fine. But it is Roddy who needs help."

Dash stiffened and inhaled before he twisted to see Roddy, who was now being helped onto a stretcher.

Still reeling from the fact that they had been rescued and by the presence of Dash, she hadn't noticed the help Roddy was receiving.

Seeing Roddy's miserable condition, Dash snarled, and then in a quick move, he smashed his giant fist into Haversham's face and then into Weber's. The men's hands were bound behind their backs, unable to defend themselves. There was a loud crunching sound when Dash's fist connected with the bones in their faces. Haversham staggered but the corpulent man, not trained like one of Haversham's boxing friends to take blows, fell flat on his back.

"How does it feel to be on the receiving end and not able to fight back?"

"Are you done, Beldon?" Rathbourne sounded bored.

"I'll never be done but I'll wait." Dash shook his fist and then lifted her into his arms. "I'm never letting you out of my sight."

A familiar voice interrupted the mayhem as the men rushed to get Weber on his feet. "Look who I discovered about to embark for

France."

All heads turned to watch Aunt Euphemia march across the dock accompanied by two very burly men who jerked a bound Lord Vinson forward. He sneered at his partners. "You fools. I should have known you weren't capable of this operation."

"It's your greed that got us here. We'll hang, but you're a fucking peer. They won't touch you." Not deterred by the blood pouring down his face, Haversham jerked toward Vinson.

"You're right. He's already sold you out. He's trying to make a deal to give us the French behind the kidnapping." Aunt Euphemia chuckled.

"My dear aunt, I told you not to get involved." Rathbourne raised his eyebrow, his tone weary. "You haven't fully recovered from your last mission."

"Cordelier, my dear Perdita was in trouble. She and Miss Rothsby needed my assistance. Mrs. Brompton is close to Vinson's housekeeper. And the poor servant was willing to betray her master. Said he packed for a long journey, told his valet he was going to France."

Aunt Euphemia poked Vinson in the chest with an umbrella she carried. "There is a lesson there for you, Vinson. Never underestimate a woman or a servant."

Perdita was never lost for words. Always quick with a fast retort, she was incapable of doing anything but stare at the elderly woman who had become so dear to her.

Concern crossed the wrinkled face, but she hid it quickly as she gazed at Perdita and her torn skirts. Aunt Euphemia stretched on her toes and patted Perdita's cheek. "Did they harm you, my dear?"

Perdita grabbed her hand and squeezed. "I'm fine. Nothing untoward happened. But Aunt Euphemia, are you… you work with your nephew?"

"That is a discussion for another time in a private place. I'm just glad you're well and being taken care of. I did warn you, Beldon. But as I said, men never listen." Aunt Euphemia's voice was laced with amusement.

"Like Vinson, I underestimated two very smart women." Dash grinned at the older woman.

"There is hope for you, Beldon." She patted Dash's arm. "Cordelier, I believe I'm finished here."

"As always, you were indispensable." Lord Rathbourne raised one perfectly arched eyebrow.

Aunt Euphemia's boisterous laughter carried across the open space as she strode across the deck.

"Take them all to Abchurch for questioning," Lord Rathbourne commanded. Turning to one of the many soldiers who must be in charge, he added, "Search the boat. Like the rats they are, I'm sure Haversham's men are scattering. Beldon, you and your men need to close down the French network before they realize they've been compromised."

Content to be in Dash's arms, Perdita didn't try to follow the conversation.

"Jones, assemble the team. I'll meet you in our usual in two hours," Dash directed a tall man with sandy brown hair too long to be a soldier. He had waved his pistol at Weber.

Roddy signaled the men carrying him to stop, so he could speak to her and Dash.

She should be embarrassed to be held against Dash's hard wall of a chest. But he needed the physical reassurance as much as she did. Also, with her back to the men, her near nakedness was concealed.

"My sister overpowered three men and dragged me to escape,"

Roddy wheezed. He held his arm across his chest to splint the pain.

Dash squeezed her, his grip almost painful. "I'm not surprised. She's always been Alfie's best student."

Dash, Roddy, and she together. Everything was right in her world. Perdita relaxed for the first time since she found herself captive. She was tired. Her brain was numb, her body exhausted. Dash's heat and the rumble of his voice and his steady heart beating against hers, with the gentle rocking of the boat, soothed her aching body and soul.

"By the familiar way my sister is allowing you to hold her, I assume that you plan to marry her?"

Dita yawned and snuggled closer. "When I thought I would die, my only regret, Dash, was that I didn't allow you to make love to me."

"Perdita," Dash shouted at the same time as Roddy.

"Darling, you're giving Roddy and Rathbourne the wrong impression." Dash smiled down at her. His eyes were soft, his voice filled with tenderness. "I behaved like a gentleman if you recall. I was a saint."

"That was what I regret." She shifted to get comfortable. She had never felt this tired. "I wish you hadn't been so darn saintlike."

Dita closed her eyes and gave over to the safety in Dash's arms. She drifted asleep to the sound of the men's laughter.

Chapter Nineteen

EXHAUSTED AND EXHILARATED from tracking down the French gutter rats, Dash climbed the marble stairs to the family rooms at Clifton house. Perdita waited for him only a few steps away. It didn't matter that she might be asleep. What mattered was that all the lies and barriers between them were gone. He could finally claim her privately and publicly as he had intended three years ago. There would be a mild scandal caused by her fast marriage to the dark lord. It would quickly fade. And despite his reputation, he was still a catch as an earl with an old title and a now solvent, vast estate.

Reese, unflagging in his duty and used to late-night activities, had reported that a resting Dr. Needham was available to give Dash an update on Perdita and Roddy. Dash didn't plan to disturb Needham or Roddy. He planned only to disturb Perdita by making her scream his name if he were a lucky bastard. Tension thrummed through his body in anticipation.

He should be at Abchurch "interviewing" the French spies that they had gathered up from the network he and his team had infiltrated. He had given close to three years of service to His Majesty in monitoring and misleading the French, and tonight was for embracing a victory on all fronts. The prisoners could wait one night to be "interviewed." And what sane man would choose hours of intimidation, threats, and lies over Perdita? After being kidnapped, almost ravished, and fighting off three men, she was adamant that tonight she wanted them to be "together."

And through the evening's work, all he could think about was a naked Perdita waiting for him. Jones smirked a few times, guessing the reason for his distraction. Hell, everyone on the ship heard Perdita's claim that she wanted Dash. He knocked lightly on Roddy's door in case his friend was asleep. Before leaving for his mission, Dash had waited until Dr. Needham had examined and reported that both Perdita and Roddy would heal. Perdita had no obvious injuries except the lump on her head from the butt of a pistol. She claimed it was nothing, and she would recover after a hot bath and a meal. Perdita was too inexperienced, but Dash knew the demons would come later. She had been attacked, threatened, and held captive, and despite her strong constitution, it would take love and support to recover. Dash planned to give all in abundance.

There was no response to his knock at Roddy's door. Dash peeked through the partially open door to catch a glimpse of Roddy in deep sleep. The laudanum that Dr. Needham prescribed was working. Dash wondered if he might find Perdita keeping bedside watch, but it was Miss Rothsby. With a book on her lap, her glasses perched on her nose, her head on her chest, she dozed. Interesting that she took it upon herself to look after Perdita's brother.

Roddy had suffered extensive injuries from regular beatings, broken ribs, a concussion, and contusions all over his body. Needham postulated that he had swollen organs from the repeated blows. Roddy's injuries were living proof of Fouche's men's brutal torture, which they delivered to an English peer on English soil.

Perdita barely escaped capture in those monsters' hands. The *what-ifs* constricted Dash's chest, making it hard to drag air into his lungs. If Perdita hadn't been trained by Alfie, if Miss Rothsby hadn't alerted them to the West Indies dock, and if he hadn't arrived in time, Perdita would have suffered unimaginable treatment by the sadists. He couldn't allow his mind to stray there, or he'd be paralyzed. The terror would keep him awake for months to come.

Dash moved silently, like any good spy, to Perdita's room. He didn't knock in fear of waking her but slowly opened the door, expecting he, like Miss Rothsby, would spend an uncomfortable night in a chair keeping watch over the patient.

His heart thrashed against his chest like a herd of thunderous stallions. An awake Perdita sat with pillows propped behind her back, her luxurious curls hanging around bare shoulders except for tiny straps of ribbons supporting a wisp of a lace bodice. All the blood from his brain drained south. Instantaneously he was hard. No finesse. His erection bulged against his breeches in blatant arousal.

"Dash." She sounded breathless, and his control teetered on the brink.

"Darling, why aren't you sleeping?" His voice came out strangled from the lack of air. Barely able to breathe or think, he was only aware of Perdita, her skin glowing, her eyes sparkling in the candlelight. He was afraid to move, or he would jump on her in a very uncivilized manner or spread her out to taste and drink like an oasis to his parched soul. He had been lost and hungry for her forever.

"I slept for hours, but now I'm awake."

Perdita scrambled out of bed and ran to him. Her arms spread open, and her wide smile lit with joy. Her excitement, familiar and yet so new, made his heart ache. Perdita was unaware of how the firelight shone through her French negligee, displaying her full, heavy breasts and the thatch of blonde hair hiding her femininity, igniting a burning inferno in him. She was a dangerous mix of fairy sprite and sensual seductress.

He stopped himself from dropping to his knees and thanking the gods for granting him the gift of Perdita. He didn't deserve her, her goodness, her beauty, and her capacity to love even his most hardened soul. He planned to love her with every breath he held to the end of his life.

He lifted her into his arms and spun her in a circle, loving the sound of her laughter, the feel of womanly contours, the satin of her hair across his chest, and the waft of her vanilla scent.

"Oh, Dash, I was afraid you were going to be noble and not come to me. I need you. I need us. I refuse to allow the leers and laughs of those evil men to take any more from me. This is our time."

Brave and clever Perdita wouldn't stew in the darkness, and she wouldn't allow him to either. She was dragging him into the light.

"I couldn't stay away. I need you too badly." He was trying hard not to push her to the wall and demonstrate his powerful need. He couldn't stop himself from flexing his hips to press against her heat. A few more moves against her soft, female folds, and he'd be spilling his seed.

She deserved careful initiation in lovemaking with tenderness and affection. Not a fast and hard ride. He had imagined this moment for three very long years, and he couldn't give in to the incessant voice in his head and in his roused body "to take her *now*."

"I never believed I would ever be this fortunate to hold you in my arms." He raised the thick curtain of her curls to kiss the silky skin on her neck. "You are so damn beautiful and so damn brave. How did I get so lucky that no other man won your heart? I followed all the news about you. It was masochistic waiting to hear of your engagement to an upright peer. When Miss Rothsby told me of your passion for a Frenchman, I was lost. Knowing I didn't deserve you, I was too selfish to ever let you go to any other man. I couldn't step away a second time. I'll make up all the hurt to you for the rest of my days."

"You were spying on me?" She traced her finger along his lower lip. "I'm going to let you make it up to me starting tonight."

He nipped her fingertip. "Nothing covert. Just the usual gossip." He didn't share how he had read all the society newspapers for any mention of her or Roddy.

Her hands came up to play in his hair at the base of his neck. "I've always been envious that you don't have curls."

Her touch was like a bolt of lightning fired down his spine, searing desire into every cell. Unable to stop, he flexed his hips and took one of her ripe nipples into his mouth and tugged through the delicate fabric. "One taste."

She threw her head back, giving full access to her exquisite breasts. The wet fabric clung to her pale pink nipples darkening them. He could spend hours on her beautiful milky breasts, teasing her until she writhed beneath him.

He exhaled deeply, trying to get his raging desire under control. His primitive male brain shouted to push her down on the bed and fill her. Men were very simple beings, unlike women who needed thoughtful words, tender touches, and affection. She was too innocent to understand her barely hidden secrets and ripe nipples in the flimsy gown shattered his restraint. He blew out another breath.

She wiggled in his arms, pressing against his erection, testing all his discipline. "Are you feeling well?"

"I'm as good as a man who is ready to combust." He pressed against her, unable to stop. "Your nightwear is not what I imagined…" He lifted her swollen breasts, weighing them between his hands. Loving her little gasps as she pressed against his hands.

"I've imagined us just like this… except my imagination can only take me so far. Take me to bed, Dash."

"Darling, I want to make this perfect for you." He carried her to the bed to lay her down gently. Before he could release her, Perdita framed his face with her hands and took his mouth. She licked at his lower lip before sucking it between her teeth. And if that wasn't enough to shoot him off like a rocket, she thrust her tongue into his mouth, searching and retreating, mimicking what she wanted. Perdita's supposed lack of imagination was quite enough.

Grinning like a madman, he reveled in her sensual attack, the onslaught of Perdita. It had always been like this with Perdita— always pushing, rushing in without weighing the risk to herself.

He lowered her without breaking their kiss. Bent over, he skimmed his fingers along the milky white skin under the bits of lace that held up the negligee. He whispered against her lips. "Darling, let me undress you."

Perdita released her hands from his hair as she reached for the fastening on his breeches. Her lips were red and swollen, her wide eyes soft with desire. "Only if you allow me to do the same to you. I've been waiting for three years to reciprocate. I want to taste you. All of you, Dash."

Dash's brain conflagrated. His hands shook, and his breath came out in uneven saws at the vision of Perdita's lush mouth wrapped around him. His voice was a series of ragged gasps. "How does a lady know of such things?"

She giggled as she scooted up the bed. "I love when you use your lordly voice to intimidate, but it has never worked on me and never will."

He loomed over her, and the scent of vanilla mixed with her

arousal filled his nostrils. She had no idea what a temptation she made, her impish grin, her curls, and all her womanly parts open and ready to be touched.

"The stable lads were discussing in great detail the skill of a certain bar maiden at the Crows Inn. They didn't know I was in the barn. And since I haven't forgotten the incredible way you made me feel, I've wanted to make you feel the same. I wanted you to be ecstatic… happy."

Perdita's desire for him broke the last barriers of restraint. Unlike other women, she didn't want to please him because he was an earl, or knew his way around a woman's body, or want his prodigious member. Perdita wanted to bring him pleasure because she cherished him. Could he love her more? And how sappy did that make him?

"Darling, we will have hours to play. I want tonight to be for you. I haven't forgotten how you taste, Perdita. Sweeter than licorice. I've dreamt of it. Shall I see if memory is correct?" He grabbed her ankles and pulled her to the end of the bed.

Her face pinked and her pert nipples jutted against the fine silk. "You can't drag me…"

She gasped when he dropped to his knees and lifted her gown for a view of her tender folds dripping with arousal. He didn't think it was possible, but he grew harder.

"So pretty and pink. You want my mouth on you, don't you, Perdita?"

"You know I do." Perdita met his eyes, no virginal modesty. He loved how breathless and needy she was as she lay back on the bed, ready for him to take. "I haven't forgotten that day."

Taking tiny love bites, then kisses to soothe along her sleek, muscular calves and then her creamy thighs, he lifted each over his shoulder. He wanted to take time to savor Perdita and her awaken-ing sensuality. He wanted to enjoy each sigh, each restless movement, each groan.

He ran his finger along her slick seam before inserting a finger. She was tight, moist, and perfect. He added his second finger, stretching her entry to ready her. He was a large man, and he wanted to give her as little pain as possible.

He bent and flicked his tongue on her engorged, hard bud; he rotated his fingers and licked her folds, avoiding the heart of her pleasure. Loving her soft groans as she writhed against his hand. She softened around his invasion.

He kept his onslaught, reveling in the sound of her every intake of breath, the tension in her thighs, and heady scent of her feminine excitement.

He wanted to delve into her heat and devour her, to have her sweet taste on his tongue. Instead, his fingers pushed in and out as he licked her bud, softly building the tension, her need, preparing her.

Perdita tightened her thighs on his neck, grabbed his hair, and shoved his head down. "Dash, please, please." Her voice was demanding, raw with need.

He wanted to shout and laugh and cry in the glory of Perdita. He took her bud into his mouth and sucked gently. "Is this what you want, my lady?"

Perdita flew, shouting his name, thrashing against his mouth. "Yes. Yes. Oh… Dash!"

Her walls tightened around his fingers, milking them as they would his member. He flattened his tongue on the spasming bud, riding the wave of her orgasm. And for the first time in his adult-hood, he felt pure joy. Giving Perdita pleasure was going to be his lifetime goal.

She fell back on the bed. Her skin flushed, and her mouth opened in an O of surprise.

He tore off his shirt and then his breeches, watching her half-closed eyes open, then widen, heating his blood to boiling point. He had never undressed for her.

Her eyes focused on his erection before her gaze took in all of him. "You're impressive."

She averted her eyes as she fingered the comforter.

"You're not getting shy now?" He teased, knowing she would rise to the challenge.

"No, but your virile body and the intense hunger on your face are quite powerful and a bit intimidating. I'm sure your ancestors looked the same as they pillaged and plundered."

He laughed in the middle of hard raging lust. He never laughed. Sex was all about release. Only Perdita would bring laughter and joy into their bedroom.

Sitting up, she yanked her negligee over her head. Her graceful and natural movement showed her complete comfort in her body and her trust in him. And he now felt like the inexperienced partner, wanting to please her.

She rose to her knees, getting close, spreading her hands on his chest, over his heart. She must feel his heartbeat thundering beneath her palm. "You're magnificent, Dash. Like the dips and curves of the marble statues at the museum come to life."

Dash stood vulnerable and open to her exploration; her honesty and admiration were humbling. She kissed his chest, swirling her tongue over his nipple. "Does it feel as good as when you do this to me?" She licked around his nipple before biting, like he had done.

"Everything about you brings me pleasure. Every touch, every smile." His voice was strangled with need and love.

Her hands wrapped around his erection, and he almost shot off.

A mix of lust and admiration of her bold ardor, he was teetering on the edge. He lifted her hands and pressed kisses to each of her palms.

"Perdita, if you touch me now, I will finish before we are joined. Will you trust me on this?"

Her skin was rosy, and her eyes filled with desire and enthusiasm for him and for their lovemaking. He had to kiss her, the girl who had won his heart. She was perfect, and soon she would be his. His. Forever.

"Lie back down. I'm afraid, my darling, that it might hurt." He lowered himself over her, not able to wait any longer. He took her mouth in one drugging kiss before he rubbed himself against her. He lifted her breasts and took each into his mouth to give her pleasure, desiring her not to suffer any discomfort.

"Now, you're mine forever." He stared into her eyes, wanting to be connected at this moment when they became one. He had waited so long and didn't want to rush. He slowly thrust into her tightness, her body opening, expanding for him. The pleasure of Perdita overwhelmed his senses, and time stopped as he drowned in her body and soul welcoming him. He kept his gaze locked on hers. Not moving, wanting to cherish and never forget this first time and the way her body and heart welcomed him.

"I love you, Perdita. I've always loved you. And always will."

"As I have you, Dash. We are now one." The awe in her voice and the way she stared down at their merged bodies snapped any vestiges of control.

He couldn't stop the urge to withdraw and thrust and thrust and thrust. "I'm sorry if I hurt you, but I promise you soon it will feel good. And if I can last, I promise greatness."

"You feel pretty great right now." She wrapped her legs around him, bringing him closer.

He quickened his pace, watching her reaction. The desire was too great, too close to the edge. He paused as his body cried out in agony. He wanted her to come with him. But he had waited for her for so long.

"Why have you stopped?" She pressed her heels into his back, her nails digging into his shoulders. "Don't stop. Not now. Please, Dash, harder." She dragged out his name, pleading.

Perdita demanding was his every fantasy come true. How could he resist her? He pushed again and then again, losing himself in the wonder. "Darling, come with me."

"Oh, Dash," she whimpered as she spasmed around him.

He growled as he filled her with his seed, releasing his love.

Chapter Twenty

D ASH COLLAPSED ON top of Perdita, unable to move, knowing his weight was too much, but he couldn't seem to make himself pull away. Enjoying the tingling of his skin and the blissful state, he floated on the waves of pleasurable release. He had reached new heights with Perdita. The woman was bold, insatiable, and proving herself to be an apt pupil in the sensual arts. He pushed himself onto his elbows to see the woman who had just shattered him with her passion and love.

With her eyes closed and a wide grin across her face, she sighed. "Oh, don't leave me. You make the best blanket."

"High praise indeed for my love-making skills." He rained kisses on her eyelids, her cheeks, and her nose.

Her eyes snapped open. "Do you need me to tell you how gifted you are? It seems with all your experience you'd be quite confident of your prodigious talents." She wiggled, pressing against his semi-hard cock, which never happened before Perdita. He was a damn lucky man.

"No, darling. All I need is you in my bed every night. I don't want to wait months for us to be together. Or sneaking around." He rolled to his side and pulled her warm curves against his chest and lifted the covers over them. "How soon can you plan the wedding?"

"The custom is to ask the lady before you plan the wedding."

"I did ask this lady." Dash trailed his finger across her collarbone and then followed the path with his lips to her sensitive and smooth neck.

"No, you commanded. There was no request. I would remember agreeing to something this important to my future."

"Perdita, don't tease me. I couldn't bear not having you as my wife." The fear of rejection after his miserable childhood tugged at his deepest fear.

"Oh, Dash. I do want to marry you."

"Then what is the problem? I want to marry you. Roddy will give his approval. Everyone will believe I married you for your dowry, the scoundrel that I am. You'll be admired for having captured the dark lord. The rumor will maintain my reputation and keep my cover."

"You plan to still be a spy?" She pushed the curls away from her eyes to observe his face.

"I will do what my country needs me to. What is it, darling? What is that look?"

"The last days have been incredibly intense and shocking. That you love me, that you are a spy. It is a lot to think about and accept."

"I've loved you since you were eight years old. I told you on our last day together. Don't you remember? I remember every second of the day. And how you came apart on my tongue, your strong thighs grasping my head, begging me. Just like you did tonight."

She gasped, her soft breasts rubbing against his chest. "You're incorrigible. What I remember is you told me you loved me that day and then came back a month later to say you didn't."

"I'm sorry, Perdita. I was stupid, arrogant, and so full of self-loathing. My legacy was a father who didn't care for me enough to secure my future. I was penniless with the responsibility to save my estates. I didn't want that life for you."

He raised to his elbow to look into her eyes. "What can I do to reassure you of my commitment and loyalty to you and you only? Tell me and I will do it. Anything."

"I want two promises sworn as a gentleman before I agree to our marriage." No cooing and soft words from Perdita. She was too innocent to use his post-coital satisfaction against him.

"Not exactly romantic, my dear." He sighed dramatically for effect. "Go on."

"Dashiell Louis Alexander West. Do not take that bored aristocratic tone." She sat up and pointed her finger sharply into his chest. "As if you're tolerating my requests."

"My apologies. I'm listening."

"Dash, please, I'm trusting you with my future happiness. I could never have a marriage like my parents. I'm not experienced like you are. There have only been random kisses and a few intimate moments, whereas you've had endless women. I've heard the rumors and have seen them with my own eyes. I know the women you've had affairs with by the way they gaze at you."

"You let other men kiss you?"

"That's your response?" She poked him again. "Yes, I've kissed other men. You rejected me without any explanation. I sought, as you did, affection and love. At least I was discreet."

He never looked for love. It was pure unmitigated lust and a need to forget. Nothing more.

"I loathe myself for hurting you and us and knowing that you turned to others because of my stupidity. But I'm here now and will always be the man you can depend on."

She ran her fingers along his cheek, staring into his eyes. "I will never be like my mother seeking affairs, but I must have your solemn oath that you won't go to other women. It would destroy me."

"Oh, darling. You can't believe that of me. How could I ever want anyone when I have you? I swear, Perdita, that I will never stray from our bed."

He gently pushed the curls away from her face as he kissed her tenderly. He wasn't any better than her selfish parents who had wounded her. But never again.

"Dash, you need to promise you won't interfere in my participation in the school and in my information gathering if Lord Rathbourne approves."

"You need to take time to heal before you can consider getting involved. You came close to dying. It will take time to forget." His mind swirled and his bowels twisted into knots at the idea of Perdita fighting for her life.

"But I'll have you to help me. I won't be alone. And I'll have my friends."

"Perdita, what you ask is impossible. I could never allow you to risk yourself. I couldn't live without you."

"And I couldn't live if anything happened to you. What you do puts you in danger."

"You know that is totally unfair." He couldn't argue that she was only a woman when she had proven how capable and strong she was. But if he didn't agree, she would resent him, and over time, she would be unhappy. Or worse, he could possibly lose her. She was a very stubborn woman. And he loved her and admired her too much not to want to honor her desires and wishes.

She sat up and pulled the sheet to cover herself. "What I had to consider doing to save Roddy and myself… I don't ever want to be faced with having to kill someone. I've searched my conscience and, like a lifeless marriage, killing another human being would devastate me. I'm trained and capable, but I only want to use my skills to teach other women to defend themselves. Each woman will have to search their conscience and decide how they can be of service. I can't make the decision for them, but I can help them find their way."

"Come back to me, Perdita." He opened his arms to embrace her as she snuggled against him, burrowing her face into his chest. "You continue to amaze me. Lord Rathbourne would never ask you to kill anyone, but you're correct if you were out in the field, you might have to deliver a mortal blow." He silently thanked the heavens above that, after having the experience fighting the French, she didn't want to take on the challenge of being an operative. He never wanted her to see the dark side of humanity even if she had all the skills to make a talented spy.

"Be honest with me. Do you think we have any chance of attaining Lord Rathbourne's approval?"

How could he disappoint her? The chances were close to nil. Rathbourne implied that he was considering it, but after Perdita's kidnapping, he would see the inherent danger of women of rank as spies, and the value to the enemies of using them as leverage.

"Perdita, if Lord Rathbourne supports you, how could your doting devoted husband not do the same? I know you'll never be content only in the role of a countess. And I don't give a damn. As long as you are *my* countess."

"How could I ever be a mere countess when I'm marrying the dark lord?"

Her laughter, like the dawning light filtering through the drapes, filled him with the promise of new beginnings.

"I'm planning on soliciting Aunt Euphemia's help in petitioning Lord Rathbourne. I still am having trouble believing she is or was a spy. Why wouldn't she tell me if she knew about our school?"

Damn. He hadn't considered Aunt Euphemia and her sway with her nephew when he calculated the chances of the school occurring. A future of negotiations with his demanding and sensual bride brought a wide grin to his face, and a feeling he wasn't familiar with and barely recognized. Contentment.

"She couldn't reveal herself. It just isn't done—to put others' lives at risk. And she wouldn't want to influence your decisions. The spy life is very isolating. You have to lie to everyone you love."

"Oh, Dash, I never thought how hard these years have been for you." Perdita propped on one elbow to look at him, trailing her finger along his jaw. "I've only thought of my pain and not what you've suffered. I had Roddy and my friends, but you were alone. Everyone believing the worst of you."

"I'll never be alone again." Dash released Perdita, jumped out of bed, and knelt. Taking her hands between his, he gazed into her eyes. "Perdita Rose Annette Tinley, will you do me the great honor of becoming my wife, the Countess of Beldon?"

Perdita rose to her knees, pressing his hands to her heart. "It would be my honor to love you for the rest of our lives, my lord."

Coming next in A Lady's School for Spies

Language of Lures

School is in session at The Lady's School for Spies and the stakes have never been higher!

Miss Emmaline Rothsby finds herself feeling like something is missing from her well-ordered life. From growing up as the vicar's studious daughter she feels like she has never truly gotten out in the world. Sure, teaching women spies how to create explosions at the Lady's School for Spies is not for the faint of heart, she still thinks there is something more out there that she is meant to do.

For Lord Roderick Tinley, life has been a barrage of smoke and mirrors. Keeping the true state of his home life cloaked behind an impenetrable veil no outsider can see through has been a constant struggle. Even his beloved sister doesn't know the extent of the abuse he's suffered at the hands of their father.

When he finds himself finally rescued after being captured and tortured by the French, he thinks that playing it safe and sticking close to home while he recovers is the best bet.

He is shocked to discover that the person wanting to help him recover from his injuries is his sister's bookwormish best friend, Emmy. Little does he know; Emmy has decided to put her books down and through a series of events finds herself embroiled in the middle of a treacherous plot.

Roddy finds himself drawn to the rebellious chemistry teacher, and when he learns she's in danger he rushes to her side.

For the adventurous couple, love is just an alluring adventure.

You can pre-order Emmy and Roddy's book.

Catch up with all your favorite female spies in
The Code Breaker Series.

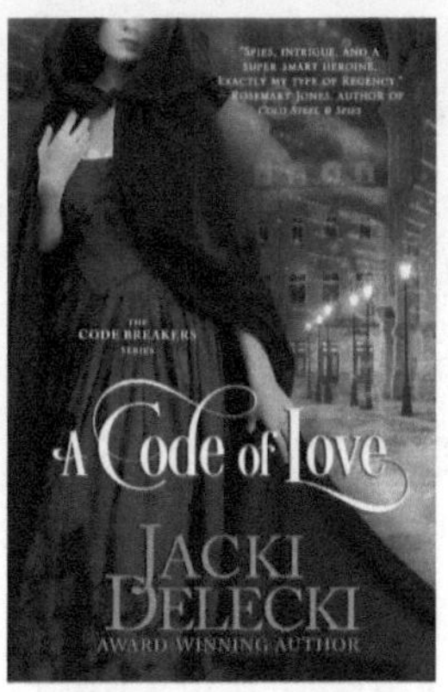

An excerpt from

A Code of Love

London, 1802

"HELP! HEN! HELP!"

Abandoning all manner of propriety, Lady Henrietta Harcourt broke into a dead run. With her muslin dress bunched in her hand, she bolted toward Edward's alarmed plea. Following the sound of her younger brother's panicked voice and the insistent barking of Gus, she darted along the rocky path to the edge of the Serpentine.

Edward bobbed in the dark water of the lake, with his dog circling and barking. Tremors of terror spread through her body, making it hard to breathe, hard to think. How could things have gone so wrong in the few minutes those two had rushed ahead of her?

The hysterical youth flailed his arms in the air.

"Edward!" Her voice thundered over the still water.

"My leg . . . tangled," he sputtered, coughed, swallowing water in his distress. His fear pierced straight through her.

Blood rushed and thundered in her chest. "Edward, I'm coming . . . I'll have you out in a trice."

She tore off her bonnet and pelisse and plunged into the frigid spring water. She walked knee-deep in the icy water toward her brother, trying hard to project calm as shock spread through her body. "Edward, I'm almost there."

The dog whined but had stopped barking.

"Hold on to Gus if you are tired."

The boy and his dog were ten feet from the shore, but the water deepened quickly. She couldn't touch the bottom after a few feet. Her dress floated around her, weighing her down. Kicking hard against her skirt, she fought to get closer to her brother.

"Edward, which foot is tangled? Can you move it at all?"

He squealed in a high-pitched voice, "I'm stuck."

Her brother's panic was palpable. She couldn't breathe, as if the glacial water were blocks of ice compressing her chest.

"Edward, give your leg a great pull. Heave as hard as you can."

Her brother remained paralyzed. His face was pale, a faint blue outline surrounding his lips.

She moved closer and stretched across the water, reaching for his arm.

"Edward, you can do this. I'll hold your arm. Pull, now."

He nodded with a whisper, "All right."

She held firm to his arm. Edward jerked his leg once, twice. "I got it, Hen . . . I got it." He was free.

"Good work, Edward. Now let's get out of this blasted cold water."

Edward started to laugh, either giddy from his close encounter or her blasphemy.

"Do you want to hold on to Gus? Or can you get back on your own?"

"I'm fine now. Come on, Gus." The boy and dog paddled across the water as if nothing unusual had occurred.

Relieved to see her brother making his way to dry ground, she started toward the shore. The effort of saving Edward and the freezing spring water had taken its toll. Her leaden arms and legs flailed in futile strokes, her movements uncoordinated. The weight of her dress dragged her down into the black water. She kicked and kicked harder. She tried to tread water, but her arms wouldn't move. The feelings of relief over Edward's rescue turned swiftly to a need to survive.

She searched the shore for someone other than Edward to help her. No one was about on the wet, cold day.

"Henrietta, come on. I'm freezing, and Gus is all wet," Edward shouted.

She considered the idea of Edward pulling her out of the water but, even from a distance, she could see him shaking from the cold. She couldn't risk his life. She suppressed the alarm darting in and out of her frozen brain.

Fighting against the ponderous dress, she struggled not to sink. Her movements became frenzied, clumsy, and ineffective. Her chest ached, and her breaths became short. She gulped, trying not to swallow the water when she went under for the second time. She heard a muffled shout but couldn't answer.

An overwhelming lethargy seeped into her, yanking her into a safe cocoon of heat. She drifted into the warm sensation. The enveloping heat was heavenly. Heavenly? Was she drowning?

She struggled against the hot steel vise closing around her. She couldn't allow herself to drown. What would happen to Uncle Charles and Edward?

Freeing her arms, she began to punch, fighting for her life. With one wild swing, her hand thudded against a hard wall.

Strong arms lifted her from the cold. "Henrietta, stop, or we'll both be underwater."

She looked up into the intense blue eyes of Lord Rathbourne—the man she detested. The man who made a mockery of all women's sensibilities.

He pushed her wet hair away from her eyes, then drew her closer to his chest. He caressed her back as he moved effortlessly to the shore. "You're safe. We're going to get you and your brother home and out of these wet clothes."

"Edward? Where's Edward?" She shifted her weight in his muscular arms.

"Hen, I'm here. Lord Rathbourne's friend gave me his coat. I'm going to ride on his horse."

She couldn't comprehend what Edward had said. It was as if her brain had frozen with the rest of her body. She couldn't stop her teeth from chattering or her body from shaking.

"My coat, Ash. We've got to get her home." Lord Rathbourne directed the man who stood with Edward.

Lord Rathbourne's companion retrieved the coat that had been thrown to the ground. Though aware of the motion around her, she couldn't focus. Edward was safe, and they were on their way home.

Hot hands rubbed her arms and legs, and then she was swad-

dled, bundled, and held securely on Lord Rathbourne's horse.
She nestled into the heat of London's most notorious rake.

Read more of Lady Henrietta Harcourt and
Lord Cordelier Rathbourne's adventures.

Dear Reader,

Thank you so much for all the support you have shown this new series. A Dash of Disguise is truly a passion project for me, and I am so excited to bring you more stories of these brave female spies engaging in espionage and falling in love along the way.

I have spent countless hours researching the time period before the war between England and France which was rife with plots to assassinate Napoleon. I wanted to weave one into my plot for A Dash of Disguise. In case you are interested, I've done a brief summary of the history that inspired me.

French Royalists devised a plot that involved kidnapping and assassinating Napoleon and inviting Louis Antoine de Bourbon, the Duke of Enghien, to lead a coup d'état that would precede the restoration of the Bourbon monarchy with Louis XVIII on the throne. The British government of William Pitt the Younger had contributed to this Royalist conspiracy by financing one million pounds. A British secret agent named Courson was arrested and under torture, confessed to the plot to overthrow the consulate. The French government arrested and executed the conspirators including the Duke of Enghien.

You might have noticed, I kept the time frame for A Lady's School for Spies the same as my Code Breakers series to have the school during the time period when England is anticipating France's invasion—to explore the lengths to which a country has to go to in order to protect its citizens. I wanted to write the stories of these courageous women and men who signed on for the challenge. I also wanted Aunt Euphemia to play a bigger part in this newest series. I hope you will enjoy her expanded role as much as I do, she is truly a force to be reckoned with.

I also wanted Perdita to be a kick-arse heroine. I wasn't sure if martial arts skills would be realistic during the Regency era. After engaging in informative discussions with the members of Beau Monde, Perdita was trained and went on to do some serious kicking. And she will continue to use her skills throughout the series.

From my discussion with my writing colleagues, I learned how female boxing was popular during the Regency period. I couldn't realistically have Lady Perdita be a boxer due to her station in society. I don't know if any of my upcoming heroines will be boxers, but it is an idea that I hope I can craft in one of the stories. I did find this intriguing article which I'll link here.

fotahouse.com/the-unbelievable-tale-of-lady-barrymore-the-boxing-baroness-boxing-and-boozing-in-regency-london

Did you make it to the end of my missive? I'll just close with this, thank you for your support for the stories and characters that I write. I honestly couldn't realize my dream of publishing without you standing in my corner, reviewing, and sharing your love for these characters and stories. Just know, I couldn't do this without you!

Thank you as always for reading.
XOXO
Jacki

About the Author

Jacki Delecki is a USA Today bestselling romantic suspense author whose stories are filled with heart-pounding adventure, danger, intrigue, and romance.

Her books consistently receive rave reviews for her bestselling suspense series: Contemporary romantic suspense The Impossible Mission Series, featuring Special Force Operatives; The Grayce Walters Series, contemporary romantic suspense following a Seattle animal acupuncturist with a nose for crime; and The Code Breakers and A Lady's School for Spies Series, Regency suspense set against the backdrop of the Napoleonic Wars.

Jacki's stories reflect her lifelong love affair with the arts and history. When not writing, she volunteers for Seattle's Ballet and Opera Companies.

To learn more about Jacki and her books and to be the first to hear about giveaways, join her newsletter found on her website. JackiDelecki.com or bit.ly/JackiDeleckiNL.

Other Books by Jacki Delecki

The Grayce Walters Series

An Inner Fire

Women Under Fire

Men Under Fire

Marriage Under Fire

A Marine's Christmas Wedding

The Grayce Walters Romantic Suspense Series 1-4

The Impossible Mission Romantic Series

Mission: Impossible to Resist

Mission: Impossible to Surrender

Mission: Impossible to Love

Mission: Impossible to Forget

Mission Impossible to Wed

Mission: Impossible to Protect

Mission Impossible to Deny

The Impossible Mission Series Books 1-3

Code Breaker Regency Series

A Code of Love

A Christmas Code

A Code of the Heart

A Cantata of Love

A Wedding Code

A Code of Honor

A Holiday Code for Love

A Code of Wonder

A May Day Code for Love

A Code of Joy

A Secret Code

The Code Breakers Series Box Set

The Code Breakers Series: Holiday Romances

Mission: Impossible Undercover Romantic Suspense Series

Undercover Danger

www.ingramcontent.com/pod-product-compliance
Lightning Source LLC
Chambersburg PA
CBHW021137190726
48288CB00008B/2708